TWENTIETH CENTURY MAN
IN AN ICE-AGE WORLD

It was a world of ice-age barbarians, clad in animal skins, defending themselves against insurmountable odds with rude stone hatchets . . .

It was a frozen world of glaciers and prehistoric monsters, a world that no living twentieth century man dreamed he could visit . . .

But David and Joan were there, plunged through time and dimension by a force they could not begin to understand. And since they were there only one thing occupied their minds —the struggle for survival!

MONSTER FROM OUT OF TIME

Frank Belknap Long

WILDSIDE PRESS

PROLOGUE

"How long will it be this time, father?" Tlacha asked, watching the tall, bearded men from the North moving about in the sunlight. She found herself wishing that her brother would come with his sacred oils and his burning, accusing eyes to make them regret what they were doing.

The tree under which she lay coiled, with her smallness giving her more the look of a child than a grown woman, had wide, spreading branches. It cast a dark shadow on her tiny feet and drawn up, berry-brown knees, and made the stooped, gnarled form of her father seem almost to blend with the swaying vegetation around him.

"How long?" he asked. "Just what do you mean?"

"How long before they leave?"

The old man shrugged. "Who knows? They give us no trouble."

"And if one of them should try to make love to me?" Tlacha asked.

"They have never done that," her father said. "They respect women."

"Mexican women, father? Indian women? What makes you so sure?"

"I am sure because my eyes are sharper than yours," the old Mexican answered. "I cannot see into the future, but neither can you. It is always veiled."

Tlacha said. "The veils are parting and I can see the vultures waiting to drop down from the sky. I know that something terrible is going to happen soon. I don't know when, exactly, but very soon."

A breeze from the Mexican Gulf was blowing across the low-lying stretch of open countryside between where Tlacha was sitting and the coastal shoreline, ruffling the hair of more than one of the toiling men and giving them a carefree, wind-buffeted look. But to Tlacha there was nothing pleasing about that look, for the workers were dwarfed by the ugly-looking machines that towered over them and

5

their bodies were spattered with clay from the subsoil that clung to them like mud.

They were of many nationalities—American, Swedish, Italian, Polish, and French—but they were all of robust build and little more than boys in years.

"They will leave soon enough," her father said. It has always been that way. They come and go, year after year. There are always new faces, new complaints. There is not enough food. They know that we are doing our best, but it is very hard to grow enough food to satisfy so many hungry men in a year when the rains do not come."

"They don't think always of food. How could you expect them to? Men have greater hungers—and women, too. Doesn't it alarm you that there are no other women here?"

"What I have just said should be answer enough for you."

"There are times," Tlacha said, "when I find myself wishing you were not my father. I find myself wishing that my mother had fallen into a deep sleep on that day, and could only remember, on awakening, that a girl child would be born to her."

Quite suddenly, the old man's gaunt body was shaken by laughter. "She was very much awake," he said. "And so was I. But if you want to believe you are the daughter of a god—"

"Why shouldn't I, if it pleases me," Tlacha demanded.

"Think whatever you wish. But your brother is a fool to believe that the gods he would still have us worship ever walked the earth. And these men will soon discover it is a mistake to dig deep into the earth to keep their own gods alive and awake. The one they call Uranium is an ugly giant who should be allowed to sleep. Otherwise he will go striding across the earth, destroying more of it with every step."

"You know exactly what nuclear fission is, father," Tlacha said, scornfully. "Why does it give you pleasure to talk like an ignorant peon?"

"It is from listening to your brother's foolishness. He lives always in the past. But there are times when it cloaks an evil that we must live with night and day."

"Should it be cloaked? If you went to Mexico City and put up a fight, the Government might stop them before our land becomes as hollow as a big, evil-smelling cheese that had been gnawed on by mice. The grease from the machines is seeping through the soil and killing a third of what we have grown. It will be worse next year and if the blasting doesn't stop I will be as deaf as you are."

"I know, I know. But I have no influence with the Government. Who would pay attention to my complaints? Our land is valuable because it is rich in many different kinds of minerals—not just uranium. Besides, I am not as angry at them as you are. They are honorable but misguided men who simply cannot grasp what the earth would be like if all life vanished, even from the sea."

A look of bitterness came into Tlacha's eyes. "We are being well-compensated for what we have to endure. Is that what you are trying to say? To me nothing can compensate for the death of one tree like this one—or for one rare and beautiful plant. Not even for just one flower growing from such a plant."

The look in her eyes remained embittered, but colored with fiery glints of defiance. "If I hawked my body in the market place like a woman from the streets, they would pay attention to *me* in Mexico City. Is that what you would have me do? Where would your family pride be then?"

"I have been stripped of that long ago," her father said. "I am very old and very tired. I want only to lie peacefully in my grave. There will be enough firm ground left for one grave."

"For two, you mean. I am both strong—and frail. That is to say, I am a woman. I can wither too, faster than any plant, even some small, inconspicuous vine deep in the jungle seeking no more than its share of sunlight and warmth. Soon there will be no warmth here at all—"

She stopped abruptly, startled by the sudden change in her father's expression and by something that she herself could hear. It began as a far-off, rumbling sound, as if a number of loose stones were falling, as they sometimes did, from one of the rock structures that arose at intervals close to the shoreline.

The first explosion was also distant, sounding more like the boom of a gun from some offshore ship than a catastrophic occurence on land. But the second blast was so loud and close at hand that it made Tlacha's eardrums ring, and the third and fourth were like the roars of two gigantic petroleum tanks exploding.

Instantly the nearest of the towering machines began to sway, causing the men working directly under it to shout frantically and scatter in all directions.

Tlacha leapt to her feet with a stricken cry, watching her father suddenly disappear, watching a great crack in the soil that had opened directly in front of her close again, swallowing him up with what seemed like a complete absence of sound. The ground where the zigzagging crack had appeared became almost instantly smooth and level again, as if nature had found so great a rupture not to her liking and had performed a miracle of surgery with no effort at all.

As Tlacha stared with her hand pressed to her throat and her face drained of all color, the tottering machine swayed more violently and crashed to the earth, sending a vast cloud of dust spiraling skyward and hiding the other machines from view.

Three men ran from the dust cloud with their clothes in flames, and threw themselves to the ground a short distance away; they rolled over and over and beat at their clothes in a hopeless attempt to put out the flames.

Tlacha started forward with the wild thought of helping them, then realized there was nothing she could do. She turned instead and began to run. She ran straight past the tree, her breath coming in choking gasps and did not stop until she reached the top of a steep, grassy elevation fifty feet away.

She swung about then and stared back, her breathing so harsh that its rasp made her feel that something was plucking and tearing at her throat-muscles with the merciless intention of ripping them apart. Suddenly just the effort of standing became too much for her, and she fell to her knees.

The smoke was thinning now and she could see that the rent in the earth that had taken her father from her had been duplicated a half-dozen times and that not all of the long, zigzagging fissures had vanished. Two of them had closed, but in so uneven a way, and with so much tumbled earth surrounding them, that it was easy to see where the cleavages had occurred. The other four were yawning, ragged-walled chasms, varying in width from thirty to close to a hundred feet. The one that yawned the most cavernously was very close to the fallen machine, which was now thickly enveloped in smoke, shot through with darting tongues of flame. Flames were also dancing about the rim of the newly-created earth crater, and a few lingering clouds of dust obscured without entirely concealing the fifteen or twenty limp bodies which had been hurled clear of the wreckage by the force of the blasts.

None of them were stirring—could a body ever stir, Tlacha wondered wildly, if no force outside of itself could bring it galvanically back to life—and a kind of instant desolation had descended on the scene, giving it an unnatural look. In the wake of a bombing the moment of turmoil which precedes such a look is usually prolonged— lasting for minutes and sometimes for hours, while people move frantically about, comforting one another, plunging recklessly through still smouldering ruins in search of vanished loved ones. But here there was only a stillness.

It had not been a bombing, Tlacha was sure of that. But it had been something almost as violent, almost as earth-shattering, and terrible in its destructive force. An earthquake? Perhaps. But it seemed more likely that it had been a man-created catastrophe, accidental and unanticipated, even by the desecrators of her father's land.

A nuclear blast? That, too, was possible. But there were other blasts that could have produced it, a linked series of charges stretching from the Gulf to where the men had been toiling without suspecting that they were laboring in Death's shadow, at the mercy of human error and human imbecility. Nitroglycerine alone could tear the land asunder, if it was stored in sufficient quantities. There was, Tlacha knew, no more destructive force on earth than a tiny grain of dangerous miscalculation germinating inside of a human skull—the skull of just one stupidly incautious man.

There was no deadlier weapon, for even if it failed to trigger a nuclear holocaust directly and by itself, it could lead to a fatal miscalculation by adversaries, equally blind, with the lightning at their fingertips.

Fortunately there were no such adversaries here, only wheeling buzzards high in the sky who would soon be descending to glut themselves on the half-incinerated, no longer living victims of a tragedy that could easily have been avoided.

But no, no, she told herself—she was wrong about one thing. She had managed to stay alive and she was determined to struggle with all of her inner strength to remain so—if no more blasts came.

Even if she had to rush about beating off the buzzards she was determined to prevent them from plucking out her eyes. No one, man or bird, was ever going to do that to her, to make her as blind as her father had been. Blind to all sanity and the great beauty of the world.

She was still swaying on her knees, gazing at the unnatural desolation that had blighted every growing plant within range of her vision, when one of the bodies moved. Slowly it lifted itself from the earth, and crawled painfully and in erratic jerks toward the rim of the chasm that surpassed the others in size.

Tlacha stopped thinking of the crawling figure as a body the instant she realized how natural it was for a man who had been felled by violence to awaken abruptly and drag himself, in stunned bewilderment, toward the first startling change in his surroundings to catch his eye. And what change could be more cataclysmic, more frightening, than a vast rent in the earth rimmed with smoke and fire?

Now he was raising himself at the edge of the crater, between two of the scattered filaments of flame that completely encircled it, and staring downward, his body grotesquely bent. It was as if he had been struck by the sudden, paralyzing thought that another cataclysm might take place at any moment and that only by staring down into the crater could he hope to find out if the earth had become still again all the way to the bottom.

Stunned and terrified as he must have been, it was an act of surprising courage and Tlacha watched him with admiration. Courage combined with presence of mind in an emergency were the two qualities she admired most in a man and just the fact that he could combine them at all after so shattering an experience made her admiration soar.

He was a very large man whom she had talked with eight or ten times, an American engineer named Harvey Ambler, from Texas—or was it Arizona?—and she had always liked him, despite the way her brother felt about Gringos and his refusal to break bread with them.

Staring at him from the high, grassy elevation, where her own safety hung by a thread, but seemed, somehow, just a little less threatened, she found herself wishing she could fly through the air to his side and share his torment, comforting him in some way before his strength gave out and he sank down exhausted. She did not want him to become a body again, to feel so cut off from all hope that staying alive would no longer seem important to him.

The dancing flames that were scattered at intervals along the chasm's rim cast a flickering brightness over the young American's smoke-blackened shoulders. But the chasm, Tlacha suddenly realized, was slowly becoming bright in a different way. A steadier glow was arising from the depths into which he was staring—a pale, almost hueless glow which was in marked contrast to the yellow surface flames. It did not flicker at all and was streaming out over the torn-up soil like a lake of light that had overflowed its banks and was continuing to spread and brighten.

There was nothing particularly alarming about the light —nothing to make Tlacha feel that another explosion was imminent and that the earth was about to be ripped asunder by a second cataclysm. Explosions seldom started that way and when they did, they were usually preceded by a faint rumbling or some other sound just as ominous.

But then, with appalling suddenness, the rim of the chasm began to tremble and a sound that was almost as loud as the blasts that had created it shattered the silence, echoing across the land to the cliff walls in the distance and reverberating back to where Tlacha was kneeling from acres of blasted tree trunks, two still untoppled machines and some metal-walled mining shacks that had survived the crumbling of the earth around them.

It was not a blast and it was far more than a rumbling. It was a clashing and a grinding, as if a dozen massive blocks of granite were falling from a great height and colliding as they fell, to land with an earth-shaking crash at the foot of a cliff from which more blocks were descending just as thunderously.

More and more blocks, colliding, falling, in an avalanche of steadily increasing violence. But it was not from a distant cliff wall that the sounds were coming, but from deep within the light-filled crater where Ambler had been lying stretched out at full length, staring down into a dark abyss which was invisible to Tlacha.

The young American was no longer at the crater's rim. But he had not been swallowed up as Tlacha's father had been. He was dragging himself away from the rim much more rapidly than he had crawled toward it, as if some great resurgence of strength and energy had come upon him.

Suddenly he was getting to his feet, with the light from the crater streaming out over him and Tlacha was rising just as swiftly from a kneeling position as the high, grassy elevation began to quake and shift about beneath her.

She did a reckless thing then. She descended to the level stretch of soil at the base of the elevation and ran straight toward him, heedless of her own safety, feeling only that if they were together when the earth opened in some other place, he would know, at least, that he was not alone.

If she had felt that way a moment before she would have thought herself quite mad. But now she had no misgivings as to her sanity. Surely there was nothing worse than to confront disaster totally alone, the last survivor in a world that was being torn asunder. At such a moment just the sound of a human voice could help, could blur a little the cruel, cold knife-edge descending. Between living and dying there was always a moment—there had to be a moment—when the anguish could be made more endurable by the presence of another. If she could do that much for him—

He saw her before she reached his side and froze for an

instant, his eyes widening in stunned disbelief. Then he was shouting at her and waving her back toward the grassy elevation from which she had descended, his voice barely audible above the sounds from deep within the earth that were becoming more and more like a series of thunderclaps, preceded by cracklings almost as deafening.

"Tlacha, go back!" he shouted. "Climb up on that slope again. The higher you get—"

But she no longer heard him, for her eyes were on the chasm now. Something was emerging from it that brought with it a different kind of deafness—a paralysis of every faculty but that of sight, as if her mind had reverted to a more primitive level of consciousness.

Her brother had once told her that man's ancestral memories went back to the dim beginnings of human life on earth and that in the depths of the mind were great beasts and writhing serpents that could return in nightmare visions, in the wild distortions of sleep. They were not physical, of course—only memory-real.

But her brother was far away now, toiling in peaceful Yucatan fields, and not standing close to a jagged chasm in the earth that was filmed with a light that had become almost blindingly bright. He could not know how awake she felt, how impossible it was for her to believe that what she saw was no more than a terror of the mind.

Out of the chasm there had emerged a great head, flat and vaguely lizardlike, even though it was covered with fur.

The head seemed more to glide than to heave itself above the crater's rim with upward-thrusting violence. But there was a violence in the way the earth at the edge of the crater was crumbling about it, as if beneath the head was so large a body that the monstrous beast could not continue its ascent from deep within the earth without completely shattering every obstacle in its path. There were clearly obstacles, for as Tlacha stared, splintered rock fragments flew high into the air and long, jagged cracks appeared in the soil surrounding the crater. One was starfish-shaped and spread over the ground in all directions, terminating in smaller craters at the end of each radiating arm. A cloud of dust arose as well, and though it

was not as dense as the one that had been raised by the
toppled machine, it caught and held the light that was arising with it and looked like a curtain of fire as it swept
across the torn-up land in the direction of the Gulf.

The great head had begun to sway now, slowly backwards and forwards as the light streamed over it, and it
was still swaying when Tlacha went stumbling forward.
She would have fallen if she had not been caught in so
firm a supporting embrace that she lost all fear of crumpling to the ground. At least, not instantly, not until the
earth heaved up again, and staying on her feet became impossible, with or without support.

Right at that moment the arms that had gone about her
seemed firmer and stronger than she had ever imagined
human arms could be. It had to be an illusion, because
however strong the man who had caught her may have
been a short while before, while laboring in the sun, the
shattering experience he had undergone should have left
him barely able to move about. But it hadn't taken so
great a toll, and just the fact that his strength seemed almost that of a giant—an illusion, surely—did not mean
that it was not a strength that she could depend on and be
grateful for.

There was nothing in the least illusionary about the
calm, confident way he was drawing her backward, away
from the swiftly crumbling and widening chasm and the
monstrous beast that was emerging from the depths of the
earth.

She knew that he was as appalled as she was, and probably as terrified. It would have been unnatural for him not
to be terrified. But there was a calmness in him notwithstanding, an inner as well as an outer strength that was enabling him to master his terror. She could feel it, sense it.
It communicated itself to her.

He said nothing, and neither did she. Movement, as
swift a retreat as possible from a horror unimaginable,
seemed the only thing that mattered, and far more important than anything they could have said to each other.

But it was the light and not the gigantic beast that pur-
sued them and overtook them and swirled about them,
blazing so brightly that it outshone the noonday sun. It

was the light that blinded them and made it impossible for them to do more than stumble about as the earth began slowly to quake and tilt again.

For a moment longer, twenty seconds perhaps, there was firmness beneath Tlacha's feet and they did not fly out from under her. Then she was falling forward, her balance totally shattered and she thought for a moment that another chasm had opened where the light seemed suddenly to become a little less blinding.

She screamed then, she could hear herself screaming and was sure for a moment that she was plunging downward. But no, no, that could not be true, for in some strange way, in the deepest levels of her mind and body, she seemed to be floating through the air and even rising. Then all sensation left her and she was neither rising nor falling but suspended in a mind-numbing abyss of leaden emptiness.

Awareness returned to her slowly, painfully, after what seemed like the passing of centuries.

She was lying stretched out at full length, with her head and shoulders slightly raised and with something hard and cold pressing against her spine. She did not know whether the something was just a ridge in the torn-up earth, or one of the shattered parts of the toppled machine—only that the ground had ceased to tilt and shift about beneath her.

She lay very still for a moment, fearing that if she tried to rise a wave of dizziness would sweep over her. It was only when she heard the sound of harsh breathing close to her that what had been no more than a small fear vanished, and she sat up abruptly.

She was not alone. The man who had done his best to make her cling to hope when no actual protection had been possible was standing less than five feet from her, swaying a little and staring dazedly about him.

On every side there stretched an unbroken expanse of snow and ice, and only in the distance was the frozen plain broken by a towering cliff wall so dazzlingly ensheated in ice from its base to its summit that it seemed encrusted with millions of diamonds of enormous size, which had been cut by some superb craftsman to bring out all of their brilliance.

The sunlight was almost as blinding as the pursuing light that had swirled up from deep within the earth in a world that had vanished. But it was not the sunlight that made Tlacha blink furiously and shut her eyes tightly for an instant. It was the bursting wonder, and the utter strangeness of what she had seen, and the need to summon enough courage, in the darkness behind her closed lids, to enable her to adjust to it, and accept it as totally real.

CHAPTER ONE

The sun was darkened, the moon hid its face
when, for a day and a night, the beast came
and dwelt amongst us. Then he was gone,
the great beast from under the world, and we
rejoiced and the sun shone upon us again.
Toltec Legend—Circa 900 AD ...

As the small Mexican fishing boat rose and fell, David Dorman could see, through the pinwheeling haze, the bare, wet, gleaming backs of the rowers, with their straining muscles standing out like whipcords in the dazzling sunlight. The oarlocks were topped with foam, and every time the boat tilted and went plunging downward, more water came sweeping over the rail to drench its eight occupants.

There was something infuriating about the way a steadily blowing wind, strong but not alarming, could turn abruptly into a near-gale, making a dangerous struggle ten times as hazardous. But what infuriated Dorman the most was the way the astounding web of circumstances which had made it possible for him to take part in so tremendous a battle of the sea was still keeping him from being little more than a spectator.

Dorman had stood up as the boat began closing in on the gigantic marine animal. The woman at his side was tugging at his beachjacket in a desperate effort to get him to sit down, her wind-whipped hair falling over her eyes and half-blinding her. He had wanted to join the helmsman at the bow and stand behind the harpoon-gun; he felt that he had earned the right, at least, to look at close range straight into the bright face of danger.

But Joan Raines would not let go. "David, listen to me," she pleaded. "You've got to listen! Do I have to stand up, too? Do you want to gamble on losing me also? Because if that's the only way I can get through to you . . ."

17

"There's no better way of making sure we'll go over the rail together!" Dorman shouted, despite the fact that a momentary lull in the wind made it unnecessary for him to raise his voice. "Just keep right on throwing me off-balance—"

Instantly she let go of his arm.

A cold fear swept into Dorman's mind; he regretted the remark immediately. He didn't want to hurt her—and God knows, he didn't want to lose her. And if it happened now—

Suddenly the tugging began again.

Dorman was so relieved that he sat down abruptly and hugged her to him. He twined his fingers in her wet hair, tilted her head back, his mouth down hard on hers. Her body moved in protest for an instant, then went limp in his arms. He was confident that this was the best way of putting a stop to her trembling.

He was careful to release her gradually. When he got to his feet again, he made sure that she would not attempt to rise by keeping a firm grip on her shoulders.

She wouldn't give in. She grabbed hold of his wrist and succeeded in dragging him down beside her again.

"David," she breathed, as the boat dipped for the twentieth time and more spray came sweeping over the rail to lash at them. "Why did we have to come out here? Why couldn't we have just stayed on the beach and watched? Why did you have to get involved with this insane expedition that might end up killing all of us?

Before Dorman could say anything in reply the boat gave so violent a lurch that she was forced to release him. He struggled to his feet again, staring out over the turbulent waters of the Gulf—blue-green where they met the sky, but almost black where the waves were cresting into foam all about the approaching sea monster.

It had seemed awe-inspiring enough on the beach when Dorman had first looked at it through high-powered binoculars. But now with the water reddening about it and two harpoons quivering in its flesh, it presented so terrifying a spectacle that it was not surprising that just its nearness had brought the woman at his side close to hysteria.

But Dorman found himself studying the creature with fascination.

It would have dwarfed a brontosaurus, and would have made the largest living whale, and the great, white man-eating shark (which has been reputed, when fully grown, to attain a length of sixty feet), seem like pygmies of the deep.

It resembled a sea-dwelling mammal more than it did a fish, for it was covered with hair of a slightly reddish cast. In fact, it would have totally lacked a fishlike aspect if it had not possessed a flaring, fanlike growth—not unlike the dorsal fin of a sailfish; this ran the full length of its body, from just below its gigantic, flat-skulled head to the tip of its massive tail.

It had four sturdy limbs, and haunches of so great a girth that they could carry a land animal over the ground in kangaroo-like leaps. But how could a land animal have resisted attack on the water with such a tremendous display of energy, or remained alive in the Gulf for very long? This creature was thrashing about where the lashing of the waves and the fury of the wind alone would have made a creature not native to the sea flounder far more helplessly than it appeared to be doing.

Still, Dorman could not quite rule out the possibility that it was actually a land animal; it could have fallen into the Gulf from some high cliff edge that had crumbled beneath its massive bulk, forcing it to swim toward a low stretch of coastline where it could disappear into the jungle again.

He was sure of only one thing. No other living creature that had ever walked the earth or made the sea its home could have blotted out so much of the sky as it leapt in pain-maddened fury from the waves of a gale-lashed sea with four-fifths of its body exposed.

Yet puny man had dared to draw close to it and was pitting all of his strength and resourcefulness against it. He was pitting as well—it was that strange mixture of curiosity and defiance in the presence of the unknown that had made him, in ages past, so triumphant a tamer of the wilderness.

There had been no need for Dorman to stand when the boat had left the beach twenty minutes earlier, watched from the clay-walled village on the opposite side of the cove by two hundred excited men and women. At a distance of close to a mile the monster had been clearly visible. Even the half-naked children who had come running out of the houses to climb on rocks slippery with eel grass could watch with wonder-widened eyes—despite the warning shouts of their parents.

The rowers, too, had been able to keep the huge beast in view as the boat moved out into the Gulf. But until Dorman had gotten to his feet the violence of the wind had caused so great an increase in the activity at the bow that he had caught only fleeting glimpses of the monster from his seated position far back in the boat.

The gale was getting stronger. For a brief moment, he found himself remembering the great winds that had roared about his boyhood home in the Dakotas, before he had gone east to major in archeology, before the untamed jungles of central Mexico. Before.

The wind seemed now to be coming as much from one direction as another, with a violence at its core that made standing almost impossible—especially with Joan's arms wrapped so tightly about his legs.

He tried to untangle her arms but the grip of the woman at his side had suddenly become so wiry and resilient that he was forced to sit down for the third time to listen.

"We may not be alive ten minutes from now," she went on relentlessly. "So I won't be silenced. You've done this before—taken wild, insane risks for no reason at all. These men are *fishermen*. They know the Gulf and endangering their lives is just routine to them. If they want to get themselves killed, all right. We have more to lose than they do."

"They have wives and children," Dorman flung back at her. "It's too late now for that kind of talk. It's hardly to your credit."

"Don't you think I know that? I've told you how I feel because I want you to be just as honest, to face up to the fact that you're being selfish and cruel! You're only thinking of yourself. You've got to realize that if this boat capsizes and the sharks find out or that creature—you're not risking *just your own life!*"

Dorman sat very still for a moment, feeling like a man who has just been stabbed to the heart without quite understanding why the wound was taking so long to prove fatal. There was enough truth in what she had said to make him not want to leap to his feet as he had been about to do, freeing himself by grabbing hold of her wrist and twisting it.

He could tell from the shouts of the rowers that the monster was shortening the distance between its thrashing bulk and the boat again. But he caught enough of what they were shouting to know that he had a moment or two left to come to terms with a part of himself that had, at various times in the past, justified the accusation that she had hurled at him.

If disaster ensued, and he sank down beneath the waves with nothing but the shadowy outlines of her face dwindling into nothingness, it would be easier if he could face up to his guilt and win her forgiveness.

And suddenly it was all coming back in great, half-blinding flashes, like images on a lighted screen when the viewer is sitting much too close.

He saw again the two-member expedition disembarking, two months previously—if one measured time by the calendar, but a wide waste of years if one were an archeologist in the pre-Columbian field descending the gangplank of a small coastal cruiser.

CHAPTER TWO

He was descending first and Joan right behind him, laden down with two heavy suitcases. He was carrying even heavier ones, and dangling from his arm was a dun-colored sun helmet which he had taken off because he couldn't stand the heat which it generated.

His slightly younger assistant and co-worker had an almost larkish look in her eyes. But he was unsmiling. Why, he wondered, when nothing had happened yet to make him feel that the jungle could be an antagonist totally lacking in sanity.

Then the jungle itself came sweeping across his inner vision, with its tropical rain forest vastness; he was a midget and so was Joan in a world of monstrous shadows.

Two crumbling pyramids overgrown with bright-colored vegetation did very little to lessen the somberness of trees that towered up for what seemed to be an astronomical distance and although at that particular moment the forest seemed empty of life, he knew that near at hand were jaguars, pumas, monkeys, armadillos, snakes gigantic in girth, and a bewildering variety of birds.

It was one of those strange, rare moments when the forest seemed totally somnolent, with just two "naked apes" moving about between the trees.

Not that he and Joan were actually naked, but they were wearing far less clothing than when they had first descended from the cruiser.

They had arrived with no first-hand knowledge of how a Mexican jungle, however somnolent, could summon ghosts from its own buried past to make itself seem a hundred times more forbidding.

His mind's eye vision ceased to embrace so wide a stretch of jungle. As it narrowed the two pyramids swept nearer and they were climbing to the summit of the one that had best withstood the ravages of time.

Then they were inside the pyramid, in a stone-walled

22

temple enclosure, staring at an enormous granite figure
that bore not the slightest resemblance to Huitzilopochtli,
the feathered Aztec war-god. It was almost formless, with
massive limbs and a flattened head that made it seem far
more beast-like than human. But it was impossible to determine exactly what it was supposed to represent because
of its lumpish shapelessness.

It was so huge and age-eroded and they had come upon
it so unexpectedly that Joan shuddered and drew close to
him, and they stood for only a moment staring up at it.
Then they went quickly out into the sunlight again, and
descended the steps of the pyramid so rapidly that Joan
lost her balance and would have fallen if he had not
caught her.

Suddenly the jungle vanished and Dorman's inner vision
became flooded with light and sound and color just as
abruptly as it had been assailed by somberness.

He was sitting on the beach with Joan at his side, drawing circles in the sand with his forefinger, and staring out
across the shining waters of the Gulf. There was nothing
to see at first but two small fishing boats bobbing about
close to the horizon. Then six fishermen came racing down
the beach to where a boat was drawn up on the sand a few
feet from the surfline.

One of them stopped for an instant to grip him by the
shoulder and point Gulfward.

He got quickly to his feet, bringing a pair of binoculars
to his eyes as the fisherman continued on past him. He did
not protest when Joan snatched the binoculars from him,
for he had seen enough. He was half-way to the boat before she awoke to the fact that he was no longer at her
side.

Then she had started to run after him, and he was turning to wave her back. But she was refusing to pay the
slightest attention to him. She had stopped briefly to pick
up a canvas bag that he had foolishly taken with him to
check over its contents while sun-bathing. He was glad
that she had done that, for though he wasn't as concerned
about the colored slides and small articles of equipment
that it contained as he was about Joan, he didn't want to
lose either. There were thieves in the clay-walled village

on the opposite side of the cove, and if the bag was left lying in plain view on the sand—

He was shouting to her now, urging her to go back, waving his arms even more frantically. But she wasn't listening. She was staying stubborn, and he was in the boat and the rowers were pushing off when he saw with horror that she was wading into the surf with the clear intention of leaping over the rail and joining him.

There were two things he could have done. He could have leapt out of the boat before it moved into deeper water, picked her up in his arms, no matter how violently she struggled, and carried her back to the beach, letting the boat depart without him. Or he could have stayed in the boat and refused to let her climb on board.

But he did neither. Instead, he urged the rowers to redouble their efforts at the oars, and it wasn't surprising that his shouts went unheeded. Probably they would have resented the presence of a woman in the boat and tried to prevent it if getting the craft well out beyond the surfline had not kept them so strenuously occupied.

One of the rowers was standing in the stern, giving the boat a final shove with an oar when Joan half-leapt and half-dragged herself over the rail and settled down in front of him, with the canvas bag between her knees. And by then it was too late to stop her without endangering her life, much less think how she was going to feel a mile from shore, when the first harpoon thudded into the monster and she experienced a compulsive need to shift the blame to other shoulders.

Suddenly there were no more swiftly changing memory flashes, only a furious conflict in Dorman's mind that made him tighten his lips in self-accusation. The reproach that she had hurled at him had been far from unjustified. On the other hand, that did not mean that his recklessness was of a criminal nature. Mixed up with the way he felt about it was a great deal of honest bewilderment. Human nature, he had always believed, was too complex to permit a man to make snap judgments about his own shortcomings. Why should a man have to castigate himself severely for surrendering to impulses that were as natural to him as breathing, impulses that had been his travelmates from childhood?

Still . . . still . . . there was a question which he felt had to be answered even in that moment of supreme peril or he might go to his death confused and self-tormented. There were better ways of dying, and no greater mistake could be made than to accept a bad death as inevitable.

Just why had he done it? Why had he gone out into the Gulf to participate in a struggle that they could have watched from the beach, as she said, through high-powered binoculars in perfect safety?

His obligation to the museum that had financed the two-member expedition? Had that been the reason? There was nothing that could increase the endowment of a scientific institution that was running short of funds more than spectacular publicity. Just witnessing at close range, as an actual participant, an occurrence so tremendous that the wire services would be humming with the news by tomorrow or the next day would be getting the drop on all of the newspapermen, from New York to Los Angeles, who would soon be arriving by twos an threes to turn the beach and the surrounding area into a jet-plane landing strip.

If he could have brought himself to believe that, if he could have convinced himself that no other consideration could have caused him to run down the beach in the wake of the fishermen and leap into the boat just as it was taking off, his burden of guilt would have been lightened. But —it would not have been true.

It had been a marginal consideration perhaps, not entirely absent from his mind. But he had gone out into the Gulf largely because there was something, deep in his nature, that made it impossible for him to resist the opportunity to experience a moment of challenging, danger-heightened awareness.

It was the kind of awareness that would not have seemed strange to a cliff-hanging mountaineer or a scarlet-caped matador. Why else would a man stand facing an enraged, pain-maddened bull in the cruelest, most primitive of all human sports, counting the danger of being gored of small moment, thinking only of how bright and magnificent the face of death could become at such a moment.

A death that you could sidestep, a death that you could defy and conquer with a dance step—one, two, quickly—and stand, amidst a thunderous ovation, proud and defiant and totally unshaken—death's conqueror for a brief moment of perfect self-fulfillment.

Perhaps the woman at his side would understand, if he bared his mind completely. But there was no time for that now, and besides, it was something he preferred to keep to himself.

In the brief moment it had taken him to re-live in memory what had taken place in the jungle and on the beach, a sea beast that could have swallowed a dozen bulls and gone right on thrashing about had apparently drawn close to the boat again, for the man in the bow was calling out to him now, his voice raised in urgent appeal.

It rose clearly and sharply above the roar of the wind, like the crack of a whiplash uncoiling.

"Señor, the woman! She must not stand! Do you hear me, Señor?"

Dorman cupped his hands and shouted back. "She is not standing. But I am coming forward."

"No, Señor! Stay where you are. You will see nothing through a drowned man's eyes!"

"Thank God, *he* has some sense!" Joan cried, tightening her grip on his arm. "Don't get up. Please, darling—please. There's no need."

The helmsman was shouting again, but his reply was drowned out by a gust so fierce that it twisted the rower in front of Dorman half-about just as he started to raise himself to increase the vigor of his oar thrusts. For an instant he could neither raise nor lower his oars, and remained motionless, his lips moving soundlessly. Then there came a wild rush of words in a half-Spanish, half-Indian coastal village dialect that made Joan clutch more frantically at Dorman's arm. "He says it's going to dive! Too many harpoons—"

"He can't be sure," Dorman muttered. "Let go of me, Joan. I've got to get past him."

"No. Please!"

"Don't be a fool. He may be right. And if he is, I've got
to make sure the gun isn't being mishandled."

Even as he moved forward—he had been relentless in
untangling her arms—Dorman was inwardly torn. Just the
thought of leaving her alone when the boat was careening
so wildly made him want to stay with her.

But he knew that he could not have saved her if an unusually big wave or violent lurch carried half of the crew
into the sea and he would be making her safety more secure if he stood with the helmsman at the bow, watching
his every movement, bringing all of the alertness of a
landsman to bear on the possible miscalculation of a man
made over-confident by the hazards he had survived in the
past.

A fisherman's luck was far from constant, and no matter how skilled the helmsman might be, another alert mind
might well be needed if the struggle took a totally unexpected turn. Or so Dorman told himself.

He had difficulty in struggling on past the oarsmen and
twice he stumbled and almost fell. Showers of spray came
swirling over the rail to lash at him, and the arms, knees
and straining shoulders of the rowers continuously slowed
his progress and came close to blocking it. The worst moment was when an elbow accidently struck him in the pit
of the stomach, forcing him to bend double for a moment
and cling with one hand to the rail.

But then, all at once, the last obstacle seemed to dissolve and fall away. He was well beyond the rowers and
standing at the helmsman's side, staring past the harpoon
gun at what seemed at first to be no more than a vast col-
umn of water spiraling skyward. It was as if the great
beast, on rising in lashing fury from the waves, had carried
a part of the Gulf waters with it, and was thrashing about
between sea and sky in the depths of a revolving whirl-
pool.

But that, Dorman was quick to realize, was largely an
illusion. The great beast *had* carried some water with
it. But it was its own, wet, gleaming immensity that had
taken on for an instant the look of a seething maelstrom
ascending straight up toward the sky.

Now all of the water was falling back into the Gulf and

the great beast stood out sharply and starkly against the sky, seeming for a moment not to be moving at all. But Dorman knew that it was the opposite of still, that its apparent immobility was also an illusion, caused by distance and the immense height to which it had towered.

And suddenly it was descending, coming straight down toward the boat before Dorman could move closer to the harpoon gun and cast more than a glance at the helmsman, who had shouted to him in warning a few moments before.

Then, all at once, the helmsman was gone. But it wasn't the descending beast that had hurled him with violence into the sea. It was the two large waves, the second higher than the first, which had come sweeping across the bow as the still sugmerged hindlimbs of the towering monster churned the water about it into a white froth, raising waves even higher than the ones that had been raising and lowering the gale-buffeted boat.

Fortunately the boat was rising again just as the waves struck it, and not quite all of the bow was submerged. Dorman was hurled sideways against the rail, and then forward to the deck. He clung for an instant to the base of the harpoon gun, slipping about and reaching out frantically for something slimmer that could be embraced, not precariously with both arms, but tightly with one hand.

He was struggling to rise and had almost succeeded in regaining his feet when the foremost rower came reeling toward him, gripped him by the shoulders and hurled him back against the rail again.

He was a youngish man, heavily bearded, and he appeared to have gone wholly mad. He was shouting something which Dorman could not hear, so loud now was the roar of the wind, and training upon him a look of fanatical rage.

Before Dorman could lift himself from the rail he was gripped about the shoulders for the second time, and found himself grappling with the man. He was almost instantly jolted by a savage blow to the temple which he managed somehow to return. He even managed to knee the maniac in the groin, but before he could break free a shadow fell across the boat and the deck began to slide out from under him. The boat shook as if it were about to fall apart and then rose high into the air. There was a terrifying kind of lightness in Dorman's chest, and though it was no different from the falling sensation he had experienced in dreams and in swiftly descending elevators, it brought with it the feeling that it might never end and was for that reason more frightening.

It was only when he found himself thrashing about in the cold waters of the Gulf, with the capsized boat drifting rapidly away from him in a tremendous swirl of foam that he realized how mistaken he had been.

The chillingly swift descent into emptiness had ended. But it had been replaced by something just as terrifying that drove all concern for his own survival from his mind.

Joan was struggling quite close to him to keep her head above water, clinging desperately to the canvas bag she had carried with her into the boat, as she might have clung to a life buoy if one had been thrown to her. Miraculously it seemed to be helping her a little, despite the fact that it had sunk quite low in the water, and could not be expected to remain afloat much longer.

A short distance away other heads were bobbing about in the water, and the Mexican youth whom Dorman had been grappling with was swimming with vigorous strokes toward the capsized boat with what was probably a madman's wild optimism.

CHAPTER THREE

When Dorman saw the great beast, a feeling of nightmare unreality swept over him. The monster was now floating almost motionless on the rising and falling waves a considerable distance from the boat it had capsized, its immense bulk almost level with the waves.

It was as if the disaster that had overtaken the boat—not its individual occupants—had freed it of all need to rear up again and inflict more injury on a shattered adversary.

It stood to reason it could only think of the boat in one way—as a small, attacking animal, an animal that for all its smallness must have seemed to it infuriating. The tiny heads bobbing about in the sea and even the vigorously swimming man no longer seemed to interest it.

Or did they? As Dorman stared, treading water and turning swiftly about with his concern for Joan seeming paramount, the strange glow that had enveloped the monster from the first seemed to expand and brighten.

All at once the light was spreading out across the water, in darting filaments of flame that looked like fiery serpents zigzagging across the gale-lashed waves toward the capsized boat and the swimming man.

The young maniac was very close to the boat, so close that he was in danger of getting his head bashed in if a rising wave brough him even nearer, when the light swirled over him.

Instantly the swimmer vanished.

Dorman started swimming then, straight toward Joan, refusing to let himself think about what he had seen until he reached her side. Just as his hand fastened on her arm the light swirled about him also.

He saw Joan's face for an instant, despite the almost blinding glare, saw the look of horror in her eyes, and the wet hair clinging to her forehead, saw the light flickering about her temples and knew that they were both caught up in it, and that escape had become impossible.

30

For an instant the glare became so bright that he could no longer see anything, and he had to shut his eyes to keep himself from being blinded. The light continued to dazzle him, burning through his eyelids, making him feel that the sea and sky were about to explode in brightness, that the earth would become as bright as the sun, a ball of fire spinning through space and that this brightness would then spread outwards until only a vast, stationary radiance remained, replacing a universe that had vanished.

Then the light went out, as abruptly as if a great hand, universe-spanning, had closed about it and all that remained was a limitless expanse of darkness.

It seemed to Dorman that he was living in two worlds at the same time. One was a world of tormenting memories that had no existence outside of his mind: a fleeting awareness of the danger Joan was in and his inability to protect and reassure her, a vast, ascending spiral of fire and water concealing a monster that his mind could no longer visualize, a capsized boat rising and falling on a tide remembered from some other age, and the despairing shouts of men sinking beneath the waves and failing to reappear.

The other was a world of moving images, some in oval and some in square frames, passing before him like a series of three-dimensional pictures projected in rapid sequence on a wide-angled screen. It was as if both the film and the projection instrument had in some strange way combined to reconstruct reality in more depth than it actually possessed, opening vistas that belonged to some beyond-time realm of being where the familiar and the near-at-hand merged with the totally unknown.

There was a jungle world not unlike the one he and Joan had explored, but the trees seemed even more immense, the foliage more impenetrable and the crumbling stone ruins had vanished. There were stone structures, but they were not in ruins and none of them were pyramid-shaped.

There was a jungle in which the vegetation was far less dense, the trees less sturdy and there were no stone struc-

tures at all. There were wide clearings between the trees
and barren stretches of boulder-strewn soil where nothing
grew, sloping down to a cold gray sea.

There was a wasteland vista where all of the trees had a
stunted and malformed look, dwarfish growths barely six
feet high, with foliage more shriveled than the withered
leaves of autumn, but still attached to the swaying
branches and still springtime green.

And there were landscapes in which cataclysmic
changes seemed to be taking place, landscapes in which
the earth remained constantly in motion, and jets of steam
were arising from pot-shaped cavities scattered at intervals
across an almost level plain.

Then, all at once, the frames separating the images
began to dissolve, faster and faster, until there were no dividing lines between them, and no sequence at all in the
way an image of one kind followed another of a totally different nature. There were green landscapes and barren
ones, coastlines that were cliff-walled and others as flat
and featureless as the pebble-strewn floor of a shallow crater on the moon.

From the first the changes had been unbelievably swift,
each image, moving or stationary, giving place to another
before all of its background features could be clearly made
out. There had been moving figures in a few of them, but
they had appeared and vanished so rapidly that they had
seemed little different from the animated, wildly gyrating
specks produced by interference on a badly-adjusted TV
screen.

But now the images were not only swift-moving but
were running together as they came and went. They were
giving birth to monsterlike distortions: shadow-shapes that
resembled gigantic beasts, huge stone faces suspended
above an abyss, long rows of jagged rocks running parallel
with a hurricane-lashed sea, the high waves cresting into
foam.

Then there was a whiteness, almost as blinding as the
light had been that had swirled about Dorman in a dimly
remembered world so many millions of heartbeats away
that it seemed to him that if he ever returned to it he
would be old and bent and horribly enfeebled; he would

be tottering on a cane or clinging for support to the arm of some pitying stranger who had rescued him from oblivion when it would have been much better if he had been allowed to die.

The whiteness did not vanish. It widened out and became even brighter and Dorman heard a voice that he recognized pleading with him. There was also a tugging at his arm.

"Darling, we're somewhere on the shore. You'll hurt yourself if you keep on tossing about. We must have been rescued."

There was silence for an instant. Then the voice went on, as if what had happened had produced so great an effect on Joan—he had no doubt at all as to his companion's identity—that she could speak no more than a few words at a time.

"The whirling has stopped. I—I didn't black out. But it was just the same as if I had. I could have been rescued by another boat, pulled right over the rail and known nothing about it. I seemed to be somewhere else, far away, with everything changing around me."

Joan's agitation seemed suddenly to increase. "Can you hear what I'm saying? Oh, darling, try. *You must try.*"

Dorman opened his eyes. For a moment he saw only the blurred outlines of Joan's face hovering over him. Then her dark hair, clinging in matted strands to her brow, cut sharply into the blurring, and when her features became just as distinct he knew that his dizziness was leaving him, and he could risk sitting up.

He sat up abruptly, surprised by his own steadiness, and his arms went around her. He drew her close and held her for an instant in a tight, unyielding embrace, saying nothing, satisfied just to be holding her. He had no idea where he was, except that the earth was firm again under him, or how many new dangers might arise in a matter of minutes that would make them feel that they had gained only a momentary respite. Perhaps even the gigantic beast might not have vanished as completely as the waters of the Gulf had when the light had swirled over them.

It was enough for Dorman just to know that Joan hadn't gone down and down into the depths and been lost to him forever. By holding her close he could make—was making—that moment last forever. He knew that some men who prided themselves on their rationality might find it hard to believe that a single moment could hold within itself all the time there was. But Dorman had always felt that the eternal had nothing to do with duration in time or space and if that meant he was irrational—the accusation would have to stand.

Joan was trembling violently but she did not seem at all like a woman who had almost drowned and who had been miraculously snatched from the sea. Her hair, which had fallen down over her face, did not press wetly against his brow and her thin clothing felt completely dry. In drying it had molded itself adhesively to her body but there was no dampness at all in the cloth beneath his palms.

Neither were his own clothes wet, as he quickly discovered when he ran one hand over his beachjacket and then over his khaki shorts.

What could it mean? Had the images that had flashed before his eyes, each in their separate frames, succeeded one another more slowly than he had thought? Or had Joan been right in thinking that they had been rescued by another boat, and that the terrible ordeal they had endured had made it impossible for them to remember the approach of the boat and what had happened afterwards. Perhaps they had been out of their minds for hours. Perhaps—

She had said that they were on the beach but there was no glimmer of water anywhere, and though his vision was still uncertain—it had grown sharp for only a moment— he was almost sure that they were surrounded by a gleaming expanse of whiteness. It seemed to stretch out for miles in all directions.

Where were they? What had happened to them?

It was Joan who told him, confessing without moving from his arms that she had lied to him.

"I didn't want to alarm you," she breathed. "But we're not by the Gulf. Darling, look—look around you. There's nothing but snow and ice—a frozen plain.

His vision was becoming sharper again, and he could see that what she had said was true. He sat very still, splinters of ice running up his spine that were just as cold, with just as sharp a cutting edge as the pendant translucencies that hung from the leafless branches of trees that looked as if they had stopped growing after reaching a height of six or seven feet.

CHAPTER FOUR

Everywhere Dorman's gaze traveled there were great drifts of blowing snow and in the far distance a gigantic wall of ice extended half across the plain, with boulders at its base so large that he would have mistaken them for small hills if they had not differed so drastically in shape. Some of them had almost the look of monoliths and others were as round and smooth-looking as the wave-polished pebbles on the beach where Dorman had let himself forget—forget that recklessness could exact a terrible penalty, when a man who had more than his own life to consider bared his throat to the knife.

He was not dead yet and didn't want to be. But if he could have spared Joan the agonized thoughts that almost had to be passing through her mind at that moment he would have let the knife go in deep.

Would it do any good, he wondered wildly, to go back to the beginning? Not all the way back to the jungle and the beach—not even his boyhood now seemed as remote —but to the moment when the sane world had vanished, and the strange light had streamed out over him? Joan in the sea, clinging to a floating canvas bag, throwing out her free arm in despairing helplessness and the monster— the monster—

Had something shaken the bedrock foundations of time and space? Had the greast beast been too massive in bulk, too towering in height to exist in the same world with the rest of nature—with ordinary animals and plants, trees and rocks? Had it been carried back through time or sent spinning through some unheard of dimension of space because it had no right to be where it was?

And had the disruption been so cataclysmic in scope that they had been carried with it, amidst some great surge of unnaturally generated light?

Just how insane was it to believe that—or even to think it?

Insane enough, surely. A dangerous kind of lunacy, and he would have put it completely out of his mind even if he had not heard Joan pleading with him to do so.

She could not have known what he was actually thinking. He was sure of that. But she was trying her best to reason her way back to sanity, to convince him as well that there had to be some logical explanation for what had happened.

He knew that he would have to disagree with almost everything she said, simply because there was no possible way of explaining what had happened that would stand up in the cold light of reason. But he was grateful notwithstanding. Somehow there was something reassuring in just knowing she shared his belief that it was much better to talk about it than to remain silent.

"This has to mean that we *were* rescued," she said." I wasn't lying to you about that, David. Do you suppose— we blacked out and remained unconscious for a very long time. And they—well, put us on a plane, to rush us to a hospital. But the plane went far off its course, and was wrecked—"

"Where, Joan? In the far north? It would have to mean the pilot disappeared and left us lying here on this ledge of rock, to freeze to death. I did think of that for a brief moment. But it's seven-ways crazy. Surely you must realize that."

"Just why is it so crazy? He could have gone to get help."

"In this frozen waste? What chance do you think he'd have? And where is the plane?"

"Maybe it came down quite a distance from here. And we struggled on together, the three of us, until we blacked out again completely. I mean, we could have regained consciousness for a short while, and have no recollection of staggering on through the snow. Why couldn't it have been that way? If we were half-delirious—"

"I'll tell you why," Dorman said. "You've overlooked something that's all-important, that practically eliminates such a possibility. You're saying that we lost consciousness in the Gulf, were dragged on board a boat without our knowledge, emerged from a plane wreck only half-conscious, and blacked out again after a long tramp through the snow. If that had happened, the odds against our both regaining consciousness again at almost the same time would be about a thousand to one.

"There's something else," he said, when he saw that she was shaking her head in stubborn denial, as if refusing to believe that the odds could be quite that high. "I was swimming toward you and had just reached your side when the light swirled over us. I didn't actually lose consciousness. Something happened that wasn't in the least like a loss of consciousness. It was like nothing I'd ever experienced before."

He stopped, tightening his grip on her shoulder. "All about me everything seemed to be changing—the sea and the land, the beach and the jungle. It went on and on. A hundred different landscapes flashed into view, and vanished very swiftly. I had the feeling it was all taking place in a matter of minutes."

Her quick intake of breath told him all he needed to know.

He remained silent for an instant, then asked: "Did you have the same experience?"

"Yes, but—it could have been—"

"I know what it could have been. But I'm pretty sure it wasn't. When you've had a great shock and start imagining things, nothing is ever quite that real. But what I'm trying to make you see doesn't hinge on how real it was. How could we have shared the *same experience* and awakened at the same time—if the impossible kind of rescue at sea and plane crackup you seem to feel could have happened had actually taken place? The odds against it would rise to ten billion to one."

It was so long before Joan spoke again that Dorman was almost sure that he had succeeded in convincing her that there was nothing to be gained by clinging to something that couldn't have brought them much reassurance —even if it had been true.

The cold was their greatest enemy. Scantily clad as they were it was hard to see how they could keep themselves from freezing for very long, even if they got up and stamped vigorously about. But that, at least, was what

they would have to do, and he waited a moment longer
only because he felt that Joan needed to bare her mind
completely. There were things that had to be said, for if
either of them began the struggle to stay alive with false
hopes, with any kind of self-deception, they would be
severely handicapped.

Things that had to be said, realities that had to be
faced, and suddenly Joan was making another attempt to
account for what had happened, clearly aware now that
her first attempt had been shattered by Dorman's relentless logic.

"David, that mountain of ice must continue on for
miles," she was saying. "It's not shaped like a mountain
exactly. It's more like the way glaciers are supposed to
look—a vertical sheet of ice, very thick, several miles in
length. Some of them, I mean. The ones in Switzerland
today look a little different, but—"

"It is a glacier," Dorman said, cutting her short. "There
can be no doubt about it. Size, shape, thickness don't
mean much. Some of them look almost exactly like enormous, snow-covered mountains. Others are much slimmer,
look like panes of glass creeping across a plain that's covered, like this one, with snow and ice, with a few bare
rocks protruding here and there.

"The ones in the Alps average about a quarter of a mile
in thickness and six or seven miles in length. But there's a
big one in the Antarctic, called the Beardmore, that has a
length of two hundred miles. There are some small ones in
Norway, but the Tystig Glacier is huge. In fact—"

The look in her eyes gave him pause.

"I know all that, David," she said. "I said I *thought*
that medium-thick pane of glass over there—if you want
to call it that—looked more like a glacier than a mountain. If you want me to change that to 'absolutely sure'—
all right. You really seem determined to dispute everything
I say."

There had been a momentary flash of anger in her eyes.
But suddenly it vanished and her arms tightened about
Dorman's shoulders.

"I'm sorry, darling. I couldn't have picked a worse time
to flare up. But I'm trying my best to think of something

that will help to explain how we got here—how we could possibly be where we are. I realize now that what I said about a rescue at sea and a plane crash was pretty far out. But it's not anything like as far out as letting ourselves believe a supernatural miracle took place. There has to be *some* rational explanation.

She paused an instant, then went on vehemently. "We could end by believing in magic carpets, by losing all capacity to reason. But I wouldn't want that to happen."

"There has to be a *complete* explanation," Dorman said, nodding. "But to find it we've got to start by eliminating everything that doesn't make sense. We've made good progress. We've narrowed it down. Now I think we're on the right track and you got there as fast as I did— maybe a little ahead of me."

"Just what do you mean, David?"

"You can be pretty transparent at times. It came to you all at once. I could see it in your eyes, even before we started talking about glaciers. That's why I rambled on a bit, to sort of—well, draw you out. It always means more when two keen, observant minds reach the same conclusion."

"I appreciate the compliment. But aren't you being just a little vainglorious."

"To hell with false modesty, Joan. This is the wrong time for it. We both have good minds—and you know it."

"And what conclusion has my good mind reached, precisely?"

"One that's just as hard for me to accept. There's been some kind of impossible-to-understand time shift and we're no longer in twentieth century Mexico. We've been carried back to an age of widespread glaciation. Just how far back in time this one was may be hard to determine. There was more than one glacial period and the last one may have been less severe than some of the others."

He was staring past her now, his eyes widening in amazement. The canvas bag that Joan had picked up on the beach was lying almost within reach of her hand. It looked as dry as her clothes were.

"You never let go of that bag!" Dorman said. "Do you realize what that fact alone would do to the complicated series of events you took seriously for a moment? A rescue at sea, a plane ride and a crackup, with a great many men concerned about you, moving you about, carrying you from one place to another. That bag would have been pried from your fingers before the plane took off, if not before. You couldn't possibly have arrived here still clutching it."

Joan had begun to shiver violently again. "David, I'm terribly cold—and frightened," she whispered, gripping his arm tightly, her fingers biting into his flesh. "If our clothes were still wet we'd be frozen by now. We can be thankful for that, I guess. But we've nothing else to be thankful for."

Suddenly she was starting to get to her feet, with the clear intention of forcing him to rise with her and face the icy blasts that were blowing toward them across the frozen waste.

In the boat she had desperately tried to get him to sit down and now she was doing just the opposite, and it angered him a little; there was nothing about an icy blast that could make a man feel that refusing to let it blow cold upon him was an act of cowardice. Not when an enormous boulder directly in front of them could provide protection, to some extent at least, from the full force of the blasts. If he had been alone it might have been quite different— would have been, in fact. He would have been out on the plain in the snow and ice, because he was a man much given to recklessness and folly.

But it was certainly wiser to remain in the shelter of the boulder until they could decide what they were going to do about finding some way of keeping themselves from freezing to death.

He took firm hold of her wrist and forced her to sit down again.

"Wait," he said. "We've got to think a little more about our most serious problem. I don't know about warm clothing. But there may be something here we can use as a substitute. Without matches there's no way we can get a fire started."

The look that he trained on her seemed to frighten her by its sternness, for she drew a little away from him. Although he was trying very hard not to let her suspect how grim he felt their prospects might become it was impossible for him to make light of a situation of the utmost seriousness—a situation that might in an hour's time—two, at most—cease to have any meaning for them.

To reassure her that he was making every moment count, that not the slightest trace of irresolution had come upon him, he raised to his eyes the binoculars that, unlike the bag, could only have sunk with him beneath the waves, for they were so closely attached to him in a water-proof case that he had not felt the slightest tugging at his waist when he had found himself in the Gulf struggling to stay afloat.

They were very light, as high-powered binoculars went, and compact as well—a truly beautiful optical instrument. But as he stared out across the plain nothing could have been further from his mind than the delight he'd always taken in precision instruments of flawless craftsmanship. He was concerned only with bringing the plain's more distant slopes as near as the level expanse of snow and ice immediately surrounding the boulder.

For a long moment he stared in silence, seeing only a flat, almost featureless series of rising and falling slopes, none of them high enough to make the plain seem other than flat when his eyes swept back and forth over it, bringing three or four miles of it into view with only the slightest tilting of the binoculars.

Then, abruptly, he lowered the binoculars, turned and touched Joan's shoulder. "There's a man in heavy furs crossing the plain about a quarter of a mile away," he said.

She stared at him unbelievingly. "David! Please don't—try to deceive me just to make me feel better. We could never be that lucky."

"There's a man out there," Dorman said. "As for being lucky—I don't know. We don't know what he's like or how he'll feel about us."

"What does he look like?"

"A big, robustly built man, about my age. Nothing unusual about him—except that I can't make out his features."

"Then how do you know he's about your age?"

It was a silly question, trivial, unimportant and Dorman knew it was only the strain under which she was laboring that had made her ask it.

"Just an impression I got," he said. "No basis for it, actually. Young or old, he could be unfriendly—dangerous. He might—"

Dorman stopped abruptly and looked at her with a strange expression in his eyes.

"Without fur garments we'll freeze to death in two or three hours," he said. "That man is wearing a fur garment and it has to mean he knows where we can get two more. But if he's hostile and refuses to help us—" Dorman hesitated, hoping that he might not have to go on.

"I know what you'll have to do," Joan said, sparing him the necessity. "It would be his life or ours."

"Only if he refuses to help us," Dorman said. "If I have to kill him to survive, I will. At least, I'll try. He may kill me. Do you understand? Does what I'm saying shock you?"

"It might have," Joan said, "if you had had a decision like that to make at some other time, at some other place. But not here, David, not in this terrible wasteland we know nothing about. We don't know how savage, primitive, brutal he may be. All right—if he doesn't actually attack you I suppose he has a right to refuse to help us, no matter how unfeeling he may be. But if he turns ugly, and you have to— Now, it won't shock me, David."

"If it will make you feel any better," Dorman said. "I may be able to persuade him to help us by struggling with him, knocking him down—"

Joan shook her head. "It won't be that way, David. It will have to be his life or yours—if he refuses to tell us how we can secure some warm clothing. Don't ask me how I know. We both know it, or we wouldn't be talking this way."

Dorman said nothing more. There was enough truth in what she had said to make him realize it was a mistake not to trust the way she said she felt about such things.

He kissed her before he descended from the ledge, held

her very tightly again for a moment and kissed her hair, and lips and eyes.

"I just won a struggle with myself, David," she said. "I was going to plead with you to just stay here, to let that man go on his way. I'd much rather freeze to death with you than be alone when I die. Then I thought how much better it would be if neither of us died and—"

"I wouldn't have listened to you," he said.

"I knew that, too, of course. And it helped me to make up my mind."

"I'll be back," Dorman said. "Don't move out from behind the boulder. I don't want him to see you."

"All right, darling. But be careful—"

It took Dorman only an instant to cross to the ledge to the boulder, encircle it, and move out upon the frozen plain. As soon as he was a few feet beyond the boulder he bent and picked up one of the many large, round stones that lay scattered about at its base.

CHAPTER FIVE

When Dorman started off across the frozen plain, with only the strength of his arms and a heavy stone to aid him if he were forced to do battle, it did him no good to tell himself that all of the legends were on his side.

All of the heroic myths, all of the glory tales from time immemorial paid homage to a man of courage fighting for his life armed only with a rude weapon, or no weapon at all. It wasn't even necessary to be a giant-killer, to be confronted with a Goliath, as the most illustrious bearer of his name had been. Just the fact that he wasn't even carrying a sling-shot and knew nothing about the nature of his adversary—how infinitely cunning and ruthless he might turn out to be—gave him the right to feel that he was holding the banners of that ancient tradition high.

But he derived no real satisfaction from the thought, no pleasure at all. How could he be sure that the man he might succeed in overcoming in hand-to-hand combat—if his luck verged on the miraculous—was not similarly unarmed? Quite possibly he wasn't a man of strength and daring, but some poor, frightened devil without admirable qualities, including good Samaritan impulses. Did that mean that he deserved to be set upon and destroyed?

To refuse to help a feared stranger, even knowing that the stranger might die, was certainly the opposite of admirable. But it was not actually a criminal act and hardly merited the penalty of death.

It took a determined effort of will for Dorman to put all such thoughts from his mind. It was necessary for him to remind himself that he would be fighting for far more than his own survival; he would be balancing Joan's life as well as his own against the life of an unknown man who, if he turned contemptible and unmerciful, would have less of a claim on survival.

That, surely, was beyond dispute. And sometimes it became necessary not to think at all—just to act. It became

45

necessary to forget that you had a conscience, to avoid a
self-destructive splitting of hairs.

There was ingrained in man an instinct for survival, as
Joan had said. And it would probably continue to be that
way until the stars fell out of the sky.

He was a third of the way to the moving figure when he
paused for an instant, to raise the binoculars to his eyes
again, and stare steadily into the distance. The man
seemed to be making a very little progress. He was
ploughing through what appeared to be an unusually
heavy snow drift and stopping from time to time to bend
over and clear a wider space for himself with an outward-
thrashing movement of his arms.

It was impossible for Dorman to determine precisely in
what direction he was heading, for he circled back once,
and started off again at a slight tangent to the course he
had seemed to be taking a moment earlier.

There were several landscape irregularities near to him
which could have provided shelter, including three enormous, snow-covered boulders and what appeared to be a
long rock structure with ragged edges, much less rounded
in shape. Its summit projected above the ice like the spines
of a gigantic porcupine, gilded with sunlight, and at its
base, which the ice did not completely cover, there were
deep fissures filled with a dull flickering. It was as if the
sunlight had been broken up into a series of tiny lights,
dancing in the depths of crevices that would otherwise
have been totally dark.

There was something strange and bleakly forbidding
about the structure that, under ordinary circumstances,
would have aroused Dorman's curiosity and made him
eager to explore it at close range. But now all of his attention was centered on the fur-clad man.

He was quite sure that the man was moving toward
some destination that was of the utmost importance to
him, a destination that was apparently hidden from view
by a sharp rise in the plain a hundred feet or so from
where he was plodding.

He had seemed uncertain for a moment as to the best
way of proceeding, perhaps because his progress had been
made more difficult by the rock structure and the interven-

ing snow drifts. But now he was moving past the rock structure undeviatingly, no longer merely heading in the general direction of the high slope, but advancing straight toward it with every appearance of resolution. It was a resolution, Dorman told himself, that he would have to match, as quickly as possible.

He lowered the binoculars and started advancing again, keeping a firm grip on the stone. It was at least a weapon but he did not make the mistake of thinking it would be of any value to him if the fur-clad man had a firearm.

A firearm? Was that possible if Joan was right and they were actually back in a glacial age? Not if she was right, of course. But how could he be sure of anything when he had been thrashing about in the Gulf one moment and in the next—or almost in the next—found himself walking across a frozen plain with his beachjacket hanging, completely dry, from his shoulders?

If they were far back in the past, would they have encountered another human being so quickly? Hadn't anthropologists in general been almost sure that in the remote past, the entire human population of the earth had not exceeded a half-million men, women and children? A hundred thousand might well be a safer estimate. Safer.

He liked that word and held fast to it. There was very little safety anywhere, but if the barren waste that stretched out before him was densely populated just beyond the rise toward which the fur-clad man was plodding, the safety factor would go down considerably. He was sure of that if he was sure of nothing else.

With the growth of human population, there had been an increase in human violence and, even in a pre-nuclear age, it frightened him to visualize the destruction that could be wrought by a vast multitude of ice-age savages, tribally united, relentless in their ferocity.

They would be much safer in a world from which human life had vanished, entirely alone amidst the frightful desolation—the last man and woman on earth. It was surely better to freeze to death than to die from a stone ax hurled with violence, or to lie stretched, still alive, over a slow fire with all hope of rescue extinguished.

But it was a bad time to entertain such thoughts and he

forced himself to think only of how close it might be possible for him to get to the fur-clad man without alerting him to the fact that he was no longer alone on the plain. He would have to be much nearer before the crunch of his footsteps betrayed him in that respect. But that would not prevent the plodding figure from turning abruptly and seeing him long before he could call out to him with his voice raised in friendly greeting.

Everything depended on that—his ability to convince the fur-clad man of his friendliness, to disarm his probable hostility before fear and suspicion sent him racing across the plain to confront an enemy who had appeared out of nowhere, swinging a rude stone hatchet perhaps, or a skull-crushing mace or some other primitive weapon, boned to a lethal sharpness.

If the fur-clad man turned and caught a premature glimpse of him, there was every likelihood that something like that would happen. Unless, of course, the man was an abject coward, and fled in wild terror, disappearing over the rise in the plain before he could be overtaken and making it impossible for a hated stranger to escape death by freezing.

But the man had not turned, and Dorman was now so close to within hailing distance of him that he was beginning to feel that his fear had been groundless.

It was a natural enough mistake and one for which he could hardly have been blamed. There are occurrences that can be anticipated. But there are others of so unlikely a nature that little thought is ever given to them—until they take place.

The fur-clad man had apparently encountered some obstacle underfoot in his slow progress through the snow and ice—a sharp stone, perhaps, that had bruised his heel or stabbed deeply into his flesh—and had swung about with his right foot raised. For a moment he had remained with his head lowered, staring down at his foot. But now he was raising his eyes and staring out across the plain.

Dorman felt all of his muscles growing tense in preparation for an encounter that he could not hope to avoid if his voice carried less far than it would have done if he had been just a little nearer. But at least he could try. Perhaps if he shouted at the top of his lungs—

But it was the fur-clad man who shouted, before Dorman could cup his palms and take a deep breath. He stumbled forward a few feet and waved his arms about and his voice was so vibrant, so emotion-charged, that Dorman was sure he would have caught every word, even if it had come from a greater distance.

"I'll be right with you. Stay where you are—or keep walking. But if you walk be careful. Ground's tricky."

He paused an instant, then went on with his voice rising, "Thank God we're not the only ones! I don't know who you are, but from the look of your clothes— A better chance now—of finding out just where we are."

It was incredible, but in a sudden flash of intuition, an agile leaping of mental hurdles, Dorman knew exactly what the fur-clad man meant. Simply, two heads were better than one. He had said "we"—so it probably meant that he had a companion too—perhaps several companions— and they could all sit down together and try to figure out exactly what had happened.

He had no doubt at all that the man who was shouting to him was an American, for his southwestern accent was unmistakable. And his words had nothing at all in common with the speech of a Neolithic barbarian, which would have been totally incomprehensible to a man of the twentieth century. It was absurd, of course, for such a thought to have so much as crossed his mind. But so overwhelming was his relief and gratefulness that he felt a need for laughter.

For an instant he was actually shaken by a kind of mirth—wild but tension-relieving. Then he was ignoring his new friend's warning about the "trickiness" of the ground beneath the ice and moving forward to join him, with so great a lack of caution that he twice came close to stumbling. Their friendship, he felt, was already cemented, already firm and unshakeable. It could happen fast sometimes, when the universe reeled and every familiar landmark exploded or vanished, and a voice, firm and concerned, spoke to you from some still surviving, small island of sanity.

It was not until he was within a few feet of his new friend that he realized just how close to a giant he was. Sturdy in build as Dorman had always been, but even as a boy more interested in scholarly pursuits than in athletics, the fur-clad man towered over him by at least five inches, and was at least one-fourth more robustly constructed across the shoulders.

His hand shot out instantly and grasped Dorman's hand in a clasp that was firm, but not in the least bone-crushing, which heightened Dorman's respect for him. A bone-crushing handclasp was something he had always resented, even in a friend, and he had never been able to figure out why it was sometimes considered a sign of warmth and goodfellowship.

"I'm Harvey Ames—from Arizona," the near-giant said. "Something pretty terrible happened. I don't think this is just the right time to talk about it. You look half-frozen, and close to exhaustion. I'd look and feel that way too—if I was wearing a beachjacket and sandals. We've got to get you into some warmer clothing fast."

"There's someone with me—just as lightly clothed," Dorman heard himself saying, feeling suddenly much colder than he had been before his new friend had called his attention a plight which only a totally naked man would have envied, and only by the narrowest of margins. There was a numbness now in his toes, but an agonizing pain was still creeping up both of his legs and across his shoulders. His lungs, too, felt constricted, and pain stabbed at his chest whenever he took a deep breath and held it for a moment.

"I'm wearing another skin under this one, just as heavy," Ames said quickly, his eyes on Dorman's beach-jacket where it had been tightly belted, and could have concealed a small weapon. "If you've a knife on you, we could divide these furs and make three garments out of them."

Dorman shook his head. "I could have made good use of a knife if you'd turned out to be what I mistook you for —a fur-wearing barbarian. I've only this stone, and it wouldn't have been much good as a weapon. I've no skill as a stone-hurler."

He showed his new friend the stone and then tossed it to the ground, where it went skidding over the ice until it vanished in a snowbank.

"My companion is a woman," he went on, turning about and gesturing in the direction from which he had come. "She's getting some protection from the wind, because she's crouching down behind that big boulder that's a little hard to see from here. But I guess you can make it out. She's waiting for me to—"

"You don't have to tell me, I can guess," Ames said, cutting him short. "She's waiting for you to come back with an expensive fur coat. There's no surer way of pleasing a woman. I've always known that, of course. But I've had it confirmed, right up to the hilt, for two weeks now. There's a woman with me, too."

For an instant his eyes crinkled with amusement. Then his expression became serious again.

"You'd have been justified in killing me," he said, "if I hadn't turned out to be a reasonably civilized coot from Arizona. No Neolithic barbarian would have parted with his furs without a struggle."

"I wasn't going to grapple with him and try to strip the fur from his back," Dorman said. "But I figured I could talk him into taking us to a hut piled high with furs where we could help ourselves. If he'd refused and turned vicious it would have been an uglier problem—"

"Sure, I know," Ames said. "I'd have hated to do it, too. But sometimes you have no choice."

"I'm quite sure I would have ended up dead," Dorman said. "So I'm glad it turned out differently."

Ames looked at him steadily for a moment. "Clairvoyance always startles me, whenever I run into it—because I don't possess the gift at all and I'm not sure I believe in it. But that hut piled high with furs— Well, it's not so wide of the mark, when you kill animals for food there are quite a few skins left over. We've been doing that for two weeks now and tossing the pelts into a deep hole we dug just outside our—I guess you could call it an igloo. We built it ourselves, out of blocks of ice."

A slight smile of amusement twisted Ames' lips again. "When pelts are uncured it's not a good idea to keep them indoors and the two skins I'm wearing stink, if I may be so blunt. But they keep me warm and they keep Tlacha warm and that's important. The ones we buried should keep you just as warm, and digging them out won't take long. New ice collects over everything you bury in half a day, but we dug that hole without letting that worry us. We just wanted to be sure warm garments would never be in short supply."

A grim look came into his eyes. "I'm not doing so well with the bow and arrow. The bow I made is pretty crude, and animals aren't too plentiful. If we run short of food staying warm isn't going to do us much good."

Ames did a startling thing then. He reached inside his outer skin, and drew out a pistol. It was a long-barreled forty-five and he jiggled it for an instant with his forefinger coiled around the trigger. "I had this on my hip when—it happened," he said. "I'm a mining engineer and I went around armed because—well, you never know. There are a few scoundrels in every fifty-man crew. I've got just three bullets left. I used the rest before I made the bow."

He returned the pistol to what almost had to be a holster strapped to his shoulder or hip, completely concealed by the fur.

"I shot a beast that looked like a gigantic anteater with snow-white fur," he said. "It couldn't have been, of course, because there are no insects here. Also a bear—a small black one with white stripes on its back. I thought for a minute it was an outsized skunk walking upright. I made the bow when it occurred to me that only a crazy man would exhaust the clip.

"Eighteen carat gold is what these bullets are made of now," he added, with a wry smile.

He straightened, his eyes traveling out across the plain again." Your companion's young, I should imagine—unless you were with a maiden aunt when the sky fell in on you, as it did on us."

"She's younger than I am," Dorman said. "We're both archeologists."

"You'd better go get her," Ames said. "We haven't far to go. The igloo's just over that almost vertical slope, right up ahead. But it isn't as steep as it looks."

He paused an instant, then said: "Archeologists, eh? In the pre-Columbian field? Was this Mexico to you before—"

He caught himself up. "We'll talk about that later. We could spare a minute or two more, I guess. But I don't want the lightning to start forking down and exploding again inside my head. Not right now. You may know something I don't, but it will have to lie fallow until we're a little more relaxed. We've got to thaw out and get a fire started first. Your sanity can slip a little, maybe seriously —if you have to keep staring at nothing but snow and ice."

He started stripping off his furs. "You can stand the cold in your birthday suit for about thirty minutes without running a risk, if you keep moving about, no matter how low the thermometer is. I mean, low within reason—not Siberian, perhaps. But I think we're having a warm spell here. I've been protected and you haven't. So your need is greater than mine. You're taking both of these skins—one for yourself and one for— You haven't told me her name?"

"Joan Raines," Dorman said. "I haven't told you mine, either. It's David Dorman."

"And you hail from?"

"The West too," Dorman said. "North Dakota. When I was a kid I used to bathe in the buff in cold mountain streams. So I was just going to tell you—one skin will do, for Joan."

"Don't be a fool," Ames said. "Your skin is turning blue."

He pushed his outer fur garment down over his knees and stepped free of it. Then he bent, picked it up and tossed it to Dorman, who caught it before it could go sailing past him and flung it over his arm. It was even heavier than he had thought it would be.

CHAPTER SIX

Ames' inner garment was the same color as the one he had taken off—brown streaked with gray—but was a little more smooth-looking, as if the animal it had belonged to had been of the beaver family, or some other amphibious rodent that had grown sleek-looking from swimming.

The gun holster—it was of black leather—dangled loosely from his hip but the strap to which it was attached had been drawn tight enough to narrow the garment a little at the waist, giving it a slightly tunic-like aspect.

He quickly unbuckled the holster and tossed it to the ground, seemingly giving no thought to what the jolt might do to the three "golden" bullets which the pistol still contained. Dorman was quite sure that there was no danger that the impact would cause the big gun to explode. But he winced a little as it went skidding across the icy surface precisely as his discarded stone had done, and came to rest close to where he was standing.

It was to Ames' credit, he felt, that the man was so intent in getting out of his inner skin as quickly as possible that he did not even stop to stride forward and pick up the weapon. It could only mean that he was a man of compassion who could visualize Joan waiting behind the boulder with her need for warmth even greater than that of a man, however thinly clad, who had been moving actively about.

Dorman was on the point of insisting, since his own need was less urgent, that Ames keep the inner skin on, despite what the latter had said. But before he could protest again the inner garment was lying at Ames' feet and he was standing completely naked on the frozen plain.

Dorman stared at him, shocked, incredulous. There were great, red-rimmed blisters on Ames' chest and shoulders and abrasions that had begun to heal, but still had an ugly look.

"I was badly battered and bruised when a ten-ton excavating machine crashed down—not on me, exactly, but close enough to hurl me a considerable distance," he said,

54

as if feeling that he owed Dorman an apology for having given him so unexpected a jolt. "Picked up a few burns, too. The flames—"

He stopped abruptly, his gaze passing from the pelt he had just taken off to something more distant at right angles to where Dorman was standing. His shoulder muscles tensed and seemed almost to ripple as though in instant alertness, and into his eyes came a look that made Dorman swing about in alarm and stare in the same direction.

The long, rectilinear rock structure was no longer stationary. It was beginning not only to move, but to change its shape as no inanimate object had a right to do. And as it hunched itself up and increased slowly in height, its ragged summit ceased to resemble a row of porcupine quills projecting above the snow and ice. It became instead fan-shaped and flaring, ribbed with spines that still arose at intervals but between which there now stretched a bandlike translucency which gleamed with a frost-crystal brilliance in the sunlight.

The snow at the rock structure's base was in rapid motion, swirling about and rising in flurries that hid the light-filled crevices that had made it seem so strange an object when Dorman had first looked at it from a distance.

Something dark and misshapen was emerging now from the surrounding whiteness, as if a snow-denuded slab of rock was thrusting the snow aside as it rose high into the air. So swift was its ascent that it had doubled in size before Dorman recognized it for what it was. His heart stood still.

The long-headed, swaying beast that was moving about on the frozen plain seemed to carry him back through time, back to the moment of nightmare unreality when just such a monster had made him feel that only the visions of madmen were real, had made him ready to believe that it was struggling to secure deliverance from its savage restlessness by devouring the universe, star by glittering star.

The great beast seemed unaware for a moment that it was not alone on the plain. It continued to sway from side to side, its head lowered, as if it had just awakened from sleep, and was searching for something to satisfy its hunger amidst the snow and ice—the burrows of a small animal, perhaps, with its furry occupant lying close to the entrance or some swift-gliding lizard, armored against the cold.

It was moving about with its huge body bent, its forelimbs almost touching the snow. But even in such a posture it towered high above the plain, and suddenly it was rising to its full height and turning slowly about.

Dorman knew when it saw him, knew the exact moment when it ceased to be unaware that two small human figures were staring at it, too insignificant to menace it in a physical way, but not in ways unknown. He could tell, he knew, even if he could not have said precisely how the knowledge had come to him.

And now the great beast had ceased to stand motionless and was coming straight toward him in kangaroo-like leaps.

It advanced so fast that for a moment it seemed like a distorted image in a mirror, with its stubby forelimbs looking even more foreshortened than they were and its hindlimbs lengthening, misting, dissolving and then growing sturdy again. Sunlight glinted on its red-furred head and cascaded over the fan-shaped growth on its back, and its long, tapering tail was enveloped in a luminous flowing. It would have been an exact duplicate of the monster in the gulf if it had not been only about one-third as large.

Dorman heard Ames shouting a frantic warning and leapt quickly to one side. The pistol was lying almost at his feet and he bent and snatched it up, freeing it from the holster with a quick upward jerk, fearing that Ames would be unable to get to it in time.

He stood very still, releasing the safety catch and coiling one finger about the trigger, watching a monstrous shadow fall and lengthen across the frozen soil directly in front of him.

He started bringing the gun up an instant before he raised his eyes, feeling that if he was about to be trampled it was better not to know, and if he could still save himself he was doing his best to make every second count.

A man could raise a gun, take aim and fire just so fast.

Trying to do it too fast meant leaving something out—usually the aiming.

He was quite sure that his aim would be good when he saw that the beast was still forty or fifty feet from him and that its bulk provided a target area several yards square.

He drew a slow, careful bead and fired.

The big pistol roared. He had fired more guns than most men with a scholarly background, but never one that buckled with such violence or tore so cruelly at the ligaments of his hand.

He was almost hurled to the ground and went reeling backwards as a thin ribbon of smoke coiled out from his hand and was dissipated by a sudden gust of wind that seemed to come rushing out of nowhere to blow cold upon him.

The great beast neither swayed nor sagged. But it could not have stopped advancing more abruptly if the air had congealed into an inches-thick sheet of ice directly in its path.

Then, slowly, it turned about, and went plunging across the frozen plain until it disappeared behind the high rise toward which Ames had been plodding when Dorman had first caught sight of him.

When Ames spoke, his utter calmness was just as amazing as the abrupt, totally unexpected flight of the beast from a single bullet that could hardly have lodged in a vital spot in a body so huge, thick-skinned and invulnerable-looking.

"It's just like the one we saw, only smaller," Ames said. "But I told you I don't intend to talk about it until we can get a tighter grip on our sanity. Take both of those skins, and put one on—right now. Then go get—Joan. Now, more than before, we've got to start moving."

He reached out and took the pistol from Dorman's shaking hand. "You did well, my friend," he said. "You saved your life—and mine. I doubt if I could have acted with one half your presence of mind. You can take that as a compliment, because I'm not exactly a slow-thinker when the chips are down.

"Only two golden bullets left now," he added, ruefully. "But I don't begrudge the loss of that one."

Dorman stared at him, his lips set in tight lines. "I'd like to return the compliment, if you don't mind," he said. "I never thought anyone could stay so calm. I feel as if the top of my skull had been blown off."

"Everyone judges a man's calmness by the control he's able to exercise over his voice." Ames said, wincing a little as if a slight barb had struck him in a spot as sore as one of the lacerations on his chest. "A lot of people have said that about me. But let me tell you something. I've no respect for a man who's incapable of experiencing strong emotion, even when it can tear him apart. In my case, it's just a deceptive personality quirk."

"It was like the beast *we* saw," Dorman said. "But we didn't just see it. It attacked—"

"As a favor to me, not now," Ames said. "I meant what I said. Going into it now would be a mistake."

The two fur garments were lying four feet apart on the snow, and Dorman picked up the one that had been tossed to him first. He had dropped it before snatching up the pistol, but now he draped it over his arm again before picking up the other skin. He had thrown the lighter garment about his shoulders, letting it dangle like a cape, and was just turning when Ames said: "You'll feel much better when we have a warm fire going and you've met Tlacha. She's the opposite of a calm woman but you'd never get her to admit it."

"Two women who have a great deal in common can usually manage to stay calmer than one," Dorman said. "They draw support from each other. As a matter of fact, in an emergency, women are tougher-fibered than men anyway. That's why they can stay so cool-headed in army hospitals or while driving around in an ambulance between bomb craters."

He thumped the skin on his shoulders. "You're getting this back before we start over that rise, no matter how close your ice-block hut may be. But you're right about one thing. I'll need it for about twenty minutes."

"You can be damned sure I was right," Ames said. "And I'm not taking it back, regardless of how often you went swimming in cold mountain streams as a kid. When I was twelve I often walked right into the sea in January, much further north than Arizona, swam for half an hour and let the sun dry me while I played basketball on the beach. And I wasn't a particularly robust youngster."

He nodded. "What I'm trying to say is—it's all in what you tell yourself. You tell yourself you can't freeze—and you won't. The human body can stand more exposure to the cold than most people realize."

"Well . . ."

"I'll just do some setting up exercises until you get back. It shouldn't take you more than seven or eight minutes.

Dorman turned and started walking in the direction from which he had come. Five minutes later he was returning with Joan across the snow.

CHAPTER SEVEN

She was the tiniest woman that Dorman had ever seen. Or so he thought for a moment, standing just inside the ice-hut. Then he remembered he'd seen two dozen or more lilliputians in his life, and of course she wasn't anything like as tiny as that.

But she was well under four feet, and ·everything about her was fragile, and delicately fashioned—from her leather-sandaled, exquisitely-shaped feet to her beautiful, cameo-like face.

She was sitting far back in the hut which he couldn't think of as an igloo—she didn't in the least resemble an eskimo, despite the warm tan color of her skin—and the dying embers of a fire banked in by a circle of small rocks cast a flickering radiance on her bare shoulders and dark, unbound hair.

Dorman turned and stared at Joan, curious as to whether or not she shared the wonder that had come upon him. He was almost sure that she did, for she was staring wordlessly and seemed scarcely to hear what Ames was saying.

Ames had been the last to enter and was blocking the entrance with his near-giant frame, as if he knew that there was no need for sunlight to stream into the hut and play around the tiny woman's head to enhance a loveliness that the firelight was aureoling in so enchanting a way.

"I'll have to ask you to forgive me again for the clumsy, abrupt way I behave at times, Tlacha," Ames was saying. "You've had so many shocks in the past few days, most of them ugly, that I should have prepared you for this one—except that it's the kind of shock that calls for rejoicing. *We're no longer alone.*"

He paused an instant to stamp out a spark that had been blown to where he was standing by a slight breeze from the opposite side of the fire, desite the fact that the hut was windowless.

Then he went on quickly: "This is Joan and this is David. They crossed the border quite recently, just a little after I did, but not to tear up your father's land. Everything they tore up was in the deep jungle—although I'm afraid that that, too, was once the property of your ancestors. They disembarked from a coastal cruiser a few miles north of your land, spent some time in the jungle and then returned to the coast again."

"But why?" the tiny woman asked, getting swiftly to her feet and staring first at Dorman and then at Joan with incredulous, far from trusting eyes.

"They're archeologists in the pre-Columbian field," Ames said. "I'm not sure you like archeologists any better than you do mining engineers. But if you could overcome that quite irrational prejudice in my case—"

He paused for the second time, a look of earnest conviction coming into his eyes. "I'm sure you won't find it difficult to think of David and Joan as friends we can depend on, friends with quite an exceptional capacity for remaining steadfast when the guidelines start fading out. I'm good at determining that kind of dependability. It can take quite a while, or occur the instant there is a meeting of minds. With me it can happen very quickly. It's one of the few compensating gifts I was born with—along with some major faults."

Tlacha was now at Ames' side, having crossed from the fire to just inside the doorway with seven or eight dartingly swift strides. Almost all of the mistrust had vanished from her eyes, but they did not leave Dorman's face as she stood facing him in the firelight.

"Where . . . how did you meet?" she asked.

"I saw him from a distance," Dorman replied, keeping a tight grip on Joan's arm that matched the one that Ames was keeping on the tiny woman's arm, feeling that there was something about the meeting that would make it seem like a confrontation until all of her doubts had been resolved.

No—that wasn't just the right term for it. It was more like a dialogue, a meeting of minds such as Ames had just referred to—four minds now instead of three, intent on achieving a total trust, a breaking down of all barriers to understanding.

"From a distance?" Tlacha asked. "Did Harvey see *you*? If he did—you were in danger. We've been living in fear—so much fear that anyone moving about in the distance would have been in danger. Harvey has three bullets left."

"Two now, Tlacha," Ames said, tightening his grip on her arm.

"Two? Then you did try to shoot him! And if you hadn't missed—"

"No, Tlacha," Ames said, shaking his head. "He saw me long before I saw him. I would have been in danger, all right, if he had been armed. He thought I was a stone age savage—"

"We straightened it out in short order," Dorman said, quickly. "He kept telling me how glad he was to see me— a fellow human being from a locality you could still locate on the map before maps became meaningless and we— Dorman found it difficult to go on. He said instead, "He couldn't have been any gladder to see me than I was to see him."

"I urged him not to concern himself with anything but just keeping warm, and getting here as quickly as possible," Ames told her. "I wanted him to meet you, and— well, there are some things it's a mistake to talk about when there's no warmth, no security, nothing that can keep you from feeling that you're standing on a high precipice staring down into absolute blackness. Or maybe something worse than blackness—jagged outcroppings that can rip and tear at you all the way to the bottom."

Joan spoke then, for the first time. "It's harder for a woman to keep her thoughts in separate compartments that way," she said. "If I was toppling right over a cliff, I'd want to talk about my chances of staying alive if I struck something to cushion the fall at the bottom. If I wasn't alone, I mean—if someone was falling with me."

She stared steadily at Tlacha for a moment. "I'm pretty sure you feel that way too. Not talking about it, not bringing it right out in the open, even if there's no warmth, no security anywhere and you may be dead before you can make much sense out of it, strikes me as foolish. So I told him more than David did, though he kept glaring at me."

"I didn't try to stop you," Ames said. "But I think it *was* foolish, under the circumstances. You see, when something unbelievable happens that makes you feel you're living in a different kind of universe from the one you've always taken for granted, you've got to try to reason rationally about it. And you can't do that if your emotions carry you in too wild a direction right at the start. You won't be able to recapture what you started off with —a willingness to believe there's a sane, sound, completely reasonable explanation for everything and the only problem is to find it."

"I told him," Joan went on, as if she hadn't heard him, "that we were attacked in the Gulf by a gigantic marine animal. We were in a small fishing boat and an attempt was being made to harpoon the monster. But it reared up and capsized the boat, and we were hurled into the sea. Then we—"

Joan broke off abruptly and Dorman was sure he knew why. A look of fright had come into Tlacha's eyes and she had begun to tremble so violently that Ames was forced to draw her closer to him and put his arm about her shoulders to steady her.

He looked at Joan angrily for an instant, then seemed to realize that she had spoken impulsively and with some justification. How could it have been otherwise, Dorman asked himself, when it no longer made sense to let experiences that must have been in some measure shared remain unexamined and undiscussed? Surely the very emotional distortions that Ames had warned against would be heightened rather than diminished by a further ignoring of any part of what had happened.

Ames was quick to make it clear that he had no intention of sparing the tiny woman an ordeal that he had probably not thought would be so difficult for her to endure, much as he may have wanted to do so.

"We've got to talk about it now, Tlacha," he said. "We've got to tell them exactly what happened to us.

Test-flight pilots have just the right phrase for it, 'Getting off the ground.' When once we're off the ground everything may be much clearer."

He gestured toward the fire. "We'd better sit down before we begin. I'll see what I can do with the fire. I told David we'd get one started as soon as we got here, but I see that won't be necessary. I'll just throw on a few more brittle twigs and we'll have a fine, warming blaze."

He nodded at Dorman, his lips twisting in a smile that seemed a little forced. "You've no idea how difficult it is to collect firewood that isn't too damp to do anything but smoulder. Or a large pile of small twigs. Big logs won't do, without an ax to chop them up with."

"How about ventilation?" Dorman heard himself asking, more concerned than he wanted Joan to know. "An indoor fire, constantly burning, should be plenty hazardous—"

"That's just it. We don't keep it burning for long," Ames said. "There's some ventilation—an updraft, I guess you could call it—from the crevices between the ice blocks. I built the igloo with that thought in mind. And the door, as you notice, can't be closed. Its just an opening cut in the ice."

"But how did you manage to build an igloo without ice-cutting tools?"

"We had a big stone ax," Ames said. "But we lost it."

He looked at Tlacha, as if he felt that talking might help to ease the strain that was still making her tremble.

"Tell him how you felt when we stumbled on it, Tlacha," he said "You were more frightened than you are now, but it didn't take you long to recover from the shock. You knew what it meant and so did I. But we agreed to think only of how lucky we were to have the tool."

"I knew what it meant, yes," Tlacha said, in so faint and tremulous a voice that Dorman had to strain to catch the words. "It meant we were not alone here. But it wasn't like—"

She looked directly at Dorman. "Meeting someone like ourselves—someone we knew and could trust. Only some primitive tribesman would have left a weapon like that lying in the snow. There were footsteps leading away from

it that were not only his. His footsteps looked like those of
a giant, but there were larger ones too—much larger. Not
human at all—"

Tlacha had begun to tremble even more violently, forcing Ames to tighten his grip on her shoulders.

He seemed to regret having asked her to speak, for
there had come into his eyes a look that verged on alarm.
But Tlacha would not be silenced now.

"It was a weapon, not a tool. It was so heavy that I
could not even lift it. And no blade of metal could have
been more sharp."

"A weapon—or a tool," Ames said quickly. "There is
no real difference, Tlacha. To the primitive mind there
were no weapons that were not also of value as tools. Or
very few."

"Only Harvey could lift it," she went on, as if she
hadn't heard him." He has a giant's strength, but he has
never used it wisely until now. Oh, I could weep for the
misuse he has put it to—lifting machines that other men
could not hope to carry, drilling deep holes in the earth,
destroying trees and flowers—"

"Tlacha feels very strongly about some things," Ames
said. "But she didn't feel that way about the ax. It took me
two days to build the igloo. The ax alone would never
have enabled me to do it. I had to rig up some primitive
leverage devices, make use of rocks and logs. But the ax
was of tremendous help. About two-thirds of the ice
blocks came ready-cut. The only problem was to transport
them and fit them into place."

"And you say—you lost the ax?" Dorman asked. "How
did that happen?"

"We left it standing outside the igloo and in the morn-
ing it was gone. I'm almost sure it was—reclaimed. It
could hardly have vanished by itself. But it's impossible to
be absolutely sure of anything in a wasteland like this. A
crevice in the ice could have opened and closed in the
night, swallowing it up. There were no footsteps in the
snow, if that means anything. I doubt if it does, for some
new snow falls almost every night, and footsteps can vanish fast."

Tlacha seemed to be making an effort to conquer her

agitation now, for she was slowly freeing herself from Ames' supporting embrace and straightening as she swung about, her eyes on the fire.

"The beast we saw—came up out of the earth," she said. "My brother would have made much of that, for he is a believer in the ancient legends. I am too, I suppose, although I went to college in Mexico City, and am what you would call an educated young lady. I even took a course in archeology, although I did not major in it. The professors there are very erudite—some of them, at least."

She shrugged. "When I returned to my father's land all of that seemed to fall from me. I became a simple girl of the soil again. I take pride in that. I have never been ashamed of what I am—or was."

"Tlacha is the daughter of an extremely wealthy landowner," Ames said. "The crew I worked with often said, jokingly, that he owned one-tenth of Mexico, at least. An exaggeration, of course. But I don't think Tlacha has ever thought of herself as the daughter of a land baron. And I respect and admire her for her ability to be, always, completely herself."

"My father was once a peon," Tlacha said. "I have never forgotten that, and I never wanted to forget it. And neither does my brother. He looks to the past where the glory of our heritage shines like a first-magnitude star, burning in the depths of the night sky."

"There is only one Tlacha," Ames said. "In all the world—only one. I'm sure of that. And despite what has happened, I feel at times that I should consider myself the luckiest of men."

"Not always—just at times?" Tlacha taunted and for a moment it was as though she had forgotten the agitation that had come upon her when Joan had told her about the gigantic marine animal in the Gulf and Ames had recalled the finding of the ax.

And now they were moving across the hut toward the fire, over a much smoother surface of snow and there was no longer any need for Ames to support her. Three skins had been stretched out on the floor, almost end to end, and it was upon the skins that they mostly walked. But there was also an icy patch and a patch of ankle-deep

snow and when they reached the fire and settled down before it Tlacha seemed to be wearing, on her tiny feet, Cin-
deralla-like slippers glittering with diamonds.

Ames bent and tossed some more brittle twigs on the
fire before settling down at her side.

Dorman put his arm about Joan's waist, drawing her
closer to him, and for a long moment they remained silent,
as did Ames and Tlacha, staring into the fire as the twigs
burst into flame and a brighter glow spread throughout the
hut.

Then they began to talk, Dorman first and then Joan
and finally Ames, while Tlaca continued to remain silent,
her eyes on the dancing flames, as if she could see in the
depths of the fire the great beast which Ames was describ-
ing emerging again from caverns measureless to man, with
the strange light hovering over it.

The fire had died down to glowing embers again when
no more questions remained to be asked or answered, and
they knew that it could only have been the great beast—or
the light—that had changed a familiar world of green hills
and valleys and seaward-facing cliffs into a frozen plain.

CHAPTER EIGHT

Dorman sat on a flat, foot-high rock in the middle of the ice-hut, shaped not unlike a footstool with a polished top. Human hands had not fashioned it, but long weathering had given it a utilitarian look and made Ames feel justified in lugging it across half a mile of snow and ice and setting it down before the fire.

It had been set down to please Tlacha, before the arrival of the guests. But it served very well as a seat, low enough to permit Dorman to upend the canvas bag without raising it more than eight or ten inches from the floor and let the contents spill out upon the largest of the two skins that had been laid down, end to end, from the doorway to where Joan and Tlacha were now crouching.

Ames remained standing, looking down at a dozen or more incredible objects coming into view. There were fifteen or twenty colored slides, held together by rubber bands, a small slide projector, less than four inches square, five or six archeological tools, apparently designed for delicate chipping or chiseling operations on stone temple walls, since they were quite tiny, and drill-shaped, a compass that looked as if it had been borrowed from a Boy Scout in the States and allowed to rust, a magnifying glass and four fairly large and intricate-looking instruments of science that were sufficiently impressive to compensate for the otherwise quite trivial contents of the bag.

"I hope there's nothing there that could explode and blow our heads off," Ames said, and though he spoke with levity Dorman was not completely sure that there wasn't just a trace of genuine seriousness in the remark. "I don't trust archeologists any further than I could hurl that stone ax I told you about."

"If it will make you feel any better," Dorman said, "I'll tell you exactly how this weird assortment of odds and ends got into the bag. We were spending most of our days on the beach and I didn't want to remain completely idle.

We took close to a thousand photographs, but there were a few slides I wanted to study more closely, under a magnifying glass. The projector was in the bag originally and I forget to take it out."

"But why the technological equipment? It looks pretty elaborate."

"That's just why I took it along. I wanted to check it over. Specialized equipment needs constant care. You don't oil the parts or anything like that. But you've got to be sure that all the intricate parts are in working order and that requires frequent inspection and painstaking readjustment."

"It would have been wonderful on the beach if he could have remained idle. It *was* wonderful, of course—but he's such a fool," Joan said. "He always has to keep busy with something. We'd run out into the surf and go swimming for awhile and then he'd forget all about me."

"Most men are like that," Tlacha said.

"I doubt if Joan will have anything to complain about in that respect now," Dorman said. "These instruments were so long in the water I can't see how they could possibly function—or tell us what I'd like to know. But we'll see—"

"What are you hoping to find out?" Ames asked.

"More about the light that swirled over us in the Gulf and that you say swirled over you and Tlacha when the beast came up out of the crater."

"You really mean those instruments can shed some light on that? Light on light, I guess you might say."

"If you want to mix your metaphors that much, go right ahead," Dorman said. "But just remember—I didn't say it. I can promise nothing."

"Just what are those instruments anyway. What are they supposed to do. I'd really like to know."

"They measure radiation," Dorman said. "In a variety of ways. One is a geiger counter that has a memory device that's like a computer attached to it. It can tell you just how strong the radiation was that started the geiger to clicking at any time in the past, even if it means going back five years. Ten minutes or five years.

"Then there's a beautiful little miniature cloud chamber, a spark chamber and a bubble chamber. And a photographic emulsion device that projects sensitive plates automatically and draws them back into itself when they've been sufficiently exposed."

"Good Lord! And you use all of this gadgetry in your work. Why?"

"There's nothing more important when you're exploring ancient ruins. By studying radioactive decay processes you can determine the exact age of many buried skeletons and artifacts. And sometimes it's important to find out if there's any radiation of a dangerous nature in certain jungle sites—"

"Apparently not quite all of our luck has run out. But I guess I shouldn't say that. Finding that ax, even if we lost it later, was a stroke of exceptional luck. It could happen again. The more we can find out about the nature of the light we saw the closer we'll be to—"

"That's jumping the gun," Dorman said, cutting him short. "I've got to find out first what the salt water may have done to—well, even the geiger. No surgeon can perform an autopsy with instruments that are all rusted away.

"There hasn't been time for the metal parts to rust," he went on, after a pause. "It will all depend on how much water soaked into the bag. Just a drop or two of salt water can ruin a delicate scientific instrument. Sometimes just breathing on it will keep it from functioning."

"You said your clothes were as dry as ours were when you arrived here," Ames said. "Had the bag dried out too?"

Dorman nodded. "I thought I told you that it had. It must have slipped my mind. But it was floating in the water for two or three minutes before the light swirled over us."

"I was using it as a life preserver," Joan said. "But it was beginning to sink."

"That's not good," Ames said. "The instruments must have become very wet."

"We'll know in a moment," Dorman said. "They seem to be in fairly good condition. It's a mistake to put too much trust in what *should* happen. It's what *does* happen that matters."

"So you've discovered that," Ames said, with a wry smile.

Dorman looked up and waved his hand. "You would all do me a favor if you went outside," he said. "The next fifteen minutes will tell the story, and when you're concentrating on the theoretically impossible it's disturbing to know that someone is watching you. It's as important to you as it is to me, and I'd be grateful, ordinarily, for the support of three sympathetic observers. But I'll be grappling with some extraordinary problems."

It was to Ames' credit—and Joan's and Tlacha's as well —that they understood instantly. Both Joan and Tlacha had to put on extra skins, but Ames had just returned from one of the twenty-minute treks through the snow in the vicinity of the hut which he took at intervals for purposes of surveillance and was wearing double skins.

He remained standing by the door until both women crossed the hut and passed out into the surrounding whiteness. Then he turned and nodded at Dorman.

"Good luck!" he said.

"Thanks," Dorman replied. "I'm going to need it."

Twenty minutes later Ames returned into the hut, preceded by Joan and Tlacha.

Dorman was no longer sitting on the stone footstool, bent above the instruments. He was pacing slowly back and forth by the fire, so deep in thought that he did not seem aware that he was no longer alone until Joan spoke to him.

"Harvey and Tlacha can stand the cold much better than I can," she said. "That's just one of the discoveries I'll probably make twenty times a day. You said fifteen minutes. But I thought we should stay outside a little longer."

"She wouldn't let us come back," Ames said. "I'm putty in the hands of an attractive woman. What did you find out? I'm almost afraid to ask you."

"Enough," Dorman said.

"I never like to hear anyone say that. It usually means the news is not good." There was concern in Ames' voice.

"It's not exactly bad," Dorman told him. "In some respects it verges on the miraculous. Two of the instruments functioned perfectly and another just limped a little while giving out information."

"If our situation were just a little less grim—I would say that a celebration is in order. We hardly dared to hope they would function at all."

"That's just it," Dorman said. "It doesn't improve our situation. It doesn't improve our situation at all to know no light on sea or land was ever as strange as the one we were exposed to. 'The light that never was on sea or land.' As a kid, when I first came across that line—it's from Coleridge, I think, but it could be from Wordsworth or Shelley—I spent long hours trying to figure out what such a light would be like. Now I know."

"But it can't be too strange—if you could break it down and analyze it scientifically."

"What makes you think that the strange, the unbelievable, can't come rushing straight toward you in the laboratory, like a high-velocity bullet. High-velocity. That may well be one part of the key to the mystery. But the key itself has been heated up, and it's too white-hot to grasp. Splintered as well, into three or four separate fragments."

"You're not making too much sense, David," Ames said, his voice sympathetic and no more than gently chiding. "Perhaps we'd better go more slowly. The light we saw was visible. I don't know very much about light in general, beyond what the average, well-informed layman is supposed to know. I'm a mining engineer, and so a little of it comes within my province."

"If you were a nuclear physicist you'd be baffled by this one," Dorman said. "God, yes—you'd be baffled. I'll try to put it simply. The instruments picked up every conceivable kind of radiant energy and infra-light within the beam of visible radiance that swirled over us. Some *very peculiar kinds* of radiant energy as well.

"Some of them would be unknown to us if they hadn't been manufactured artificially by nuclear reactors. Others defied analysis, but showed up in one or two characteristic lines associated with what must be closely related forms. Every radioactive process that can be imagined as taking place in space or on the planets of the Solar System must have existed within that light.

"There were a tremendous number of bare atomic nuclei, but not all of these high-energy particles were identical with cosmic rays as we know them, or even identical with the cosmic rays of galactic origin which have left fission tracks in meteorites."

"What are you trying to tell me?" Ames asked.

Both Joan and Tlacha had moved close to Dorman, and were looking at him almost pleadingly, as if they shared both Ames' bewilderment and his increasing impatience.

"We know what a controlling environmental influence vegetation exerts, how all animal life as we know it would face extinction if all plant life should vanish from the earth. What if the beast came from some region where radiant energies have taken the place of vegetation? Some region of matter-binding energies ceasing to bind, exploding in high-velocity particles on a tremendous scale. Every form of energy and visible and invisible light, enabling the beast to develop peculiarities, in relation to such an environment, that would shake the keystone of matter itself if it emerged from a world natural to it deep within the earth."

"Hold on a minute, David," Ames said. "Would just what you've found out about the light, startling as it may be, justify—well, building a superstructure to account for it that strains credulity to that extent? All we actually know about the beast is that it emerged from a dynamite-blasted crater and then must have plunged—or fallen—into the Gulf."

"I'm far from sure it hasn't happened before," Dorman said." A prehistoric monster, appearing suddenly in the jungle, causing unimaginable havoc. Right after a volcanic eruption, perhaps. There is no mention of such an occurrence in Aztec mythology, but there are Toltec and Mayan legends in which it becomes almost a central myth, from about the seventh to the tenth centuries. The Toltecs had a profound influence on Mayan civilization, but the Mayans worshipped so many other gods, of rain, wind and fertility, as well as animals and snakes, that the prehistoric monster legend became swallowed up. But you can find it if you search."

"Something that bore an unmistakable resemblance to a

great beast was standing in a temple ruin we explored,"
Joan said. "It was carved out of quartz sandstone and a
part of it had crumbled away. We didn't stay there long."

"All right," Ames said. "Let's forget about the Toltecs
for a moment. If you're searching for legends, the Mino-
taur might not be so different from the beast we saw. It
must have been huge, to frighten kids for more than two
thousand years."

"Four thousand, most likely," Dorman said. "It was a
Trojan myth before it was taken over by the Greeks."

"All right, I stand corrected.

He looked at Dorman steadily for a moment, all of the
levity going out of his eyes.

"I might be able to buy a little of what you just said—
about a region where there are tremendous, nuclear chain
reactions going on all the time, making uranium fission
look like an ember from our fire that takes half the night
to burn itself out. Do you seriously believe in a hollow
world—that there could actually be such a region under
the earth's crust?"

"I didn't, before the sky fell in on us, as you put it when
we first met. I'm far from sure I do now. That monster
could have come from—some other dimension of space-
time, another part of the continuum—call it whatever you
wish. We know nothing whatever about higher-dimen-
sional worlds, because we've never had the slightest reason
to believe that they exist."

"It would be much easier," Ames said, "to believe that
some gigantic prehistoric animal, the last of its species, fell
by accident into a cavern in the deep jungle and remained
trapped underground until the mining accident enabled it
to escape through a blast-widened tunnel. A creature seldom seen by human eyes, never emerging from the
jungle."

"Perhaps that isn't so wide of the mark," Dorman said.
"Something like that may have happened—a half million
or two million years ago. A beast ancestral to the one we
saw may have become trapped in precisely that way in the
remote past, and natural selection enabled its descendants
to survive in a subterranean world with no vegetation, a

world of radiant energy. Two beasts, of course—a male and a female. Long ages of adaptation, of mutational changes, may have turned the beast we saw, and others of its kind into energy-generating monsters.

"If we can keep nuclear explosions bottled up deep underground why should it be so hard to believe that there may be some region, deep within the earth, where radioactive atoms create trillions upon trillions of electron volts, not slowly through a process of radioactive decay but swiftly and constantly?"

"Standing alone, it might not be too hard to believe. But you've hinted at something that places a much greater strain on credulity," Ames said. "I may be mistaken. But you seem willing to believe that such a monster could not reappear on the surface of the earth without shattering, to some extent at least, the binding energies of matter in a more fundamental or relativistic way—in the actual relationship which space bears to time. You seem willing to believe that, in some unfathomable way, a small segment of the space-time continuum was ripped apart and we were carried back into the past."

Dorman started to say something in reply, but the other gestured him to silence. "Please, David—hear me out. Are you seriously claiming that the light that swirled over us could do that, could carry us back through a succession of swiftly dissolving—I guess you could call them time-frames—to the last glacial age, or perhaps an earlier one? Without destroying us? How could we survive even a few minutes exposure to such radiation?"

"I do not know," Dorman said. "But it's far from inconceivable that we were shielded in some way from the radiation itself, that only the waters of the Gulf immediately surrounding us—in your case, the land—underwent a time shift, carrying us with them into the past.

"A ship at sea can remain becalmed and perfectly stationary at the center of a gigantic storm wind. At the core of every hurricane there is a region of absolute calm. But if the storm wind should swirl up and leave the earth— which of course it could not do—would it not be very likely to carry the ship with it?

"A lightning bolt can behave in just as freakish a way—blast a tree under which a man is standing, rip all the clothes from his body and not harm a hair of his head."

"But the instruments in that canvas bag picked up the radiation. Joan said she was clinging to it—"

"Instruments of science are quite different from human beings," Dorman said. "They can both behave freakishly at times, but a precision instrument is unlikely to have quite as high a capacity to trade on its luck. It just happened, that's all. The radiation was picked up sporadically, unevenly and not as accurately as I could have wished. It was recorded only once as sufficiently lethal to have destroyed us instantly."

Joan spoke then, for the second time, and though her voice had been tremulous before, Dorman had been too preoccupied with what the instruments had revealed to realize she was in need of reassurance. But her words made him aware of that need to such an extent that nothing else seemed, for an instant, to be of the slightest importance.

"How can we be sure we *haven't* been exposed to a dangerous amount of radiation?" she asked. "Would we know, instantly—or even after a week, or a month? What if a year from now—"

"We'd know, if it was really bad," Dorman said, putting his arm about her and drawing her close to him. "There are no burns—nothing. But I intend to check on it, of course. These instruments will tell us."

For the next hour and a half the ice-hut became a kind of medical clinic. Dorman had never before assumed the role of a physician and he felt a little awkward conducting tests that made it necessary for him to ask Ames, Tlacha and Joan to remove all of their clothes.

Ames had thrown more twigs on the fire, and each of them undressed separately and put their skins back on again the instant Dorman was satisfied that he could do no more to enable them to sleep soundly all night long, without the restless tossing about that would have been inevitable if they had entertained serious doubts as to their freedom from the slightest evidence of radioactivity.

At least, they were not radioactive, as the geiger quickly demonstrated. But there were other tests that had to be made, and a few lingering doubts remained in Dorman's mind as to the absolute accuracy of his diagnosis. Even an exposure that had not left them radioactive might prove to have been an unfortunate occurrence several years in the future. But he did not think that it would turn out that way and he was careful to keep all of his misgivings—and they were very slight ones—to himself.

CHAPTER NINE

Joan awoke with a start, thinking for a moment that she had heard someone—or something—moving about outside the hut. But probably, she told herself, she had been mistaken. The thought of getting up and awakening Dorman she dismissed at once. He had sat up most of the night and had fallen now into a deep sleep, a short distance from where Ames and Tlacha were sleeping a few feet apart, wrapped, as she and Dorman were, in heavy furs.

Joan would not have been at all surprised—certainly not shocked—if they had been sleeping coiled up in each other's arms. The presence of two strangers—friends now, of course—might have made such a display of intimacy seem embarrassing and in bad taste if they had been week-end guests at a crowded "house party," forced to sleep in the same room because guest rooms were at a premium.

But in view of where they were and how long it might be before they found themselves in a house again it was madness to expect them to constantly conceal the extent to which their love-making had progressed.

She was almost certain that it had progressed as far as it could go. They had been living a hair's breadth from annihilation for more than two weeks, had shared undreamed of hazards, had been thrown together night and day. And what Ames had said about Tlacha had made it unmistakably plain that he was just about as love-smitten as a man could be.

He was either madly in love with her, or found her so attractive that if he had been asked to choose between Tlacha and a hundred other women there could be little doubt as to what his choice would have been.

Joan suddenly realized that she would have been neither shocked nor too much surprised if he had lowered

the skin over Tlacha's shoulder and fallen asleep with his
head cradled against her bare flesh.

She realized as well that she would have resented, under
ordinary circumstances, being forced to be a participant in
such an act of intimacy, particularly in the presence of a
man whom she loved. Just being present and visually
aware of what was taking place would have made her, in a
sense, a participant.

She had never believed in what went on among certain
married couples who dismissed conventional reticence as
hypocritical and were always talking about the new group
"permissiveness."

But that did not mean that there were not circumstances which could alter, temporarily, the way you felt
about almost everything. Human nature could endure just
so much constraint and a man and woman who thought
that the next moment—or the one after that—might very
well be their last could hardly be blamed for abandoning
constraint. A man could hardly be blamed for taking a
woman who had become very precious to him into his
arms and crushing her to him and making passionate love
to her, even in the presence of others.

Barriers to observation could usually be erected, of
course, even an ice-hut curtained off, a veil drawn over
what was taking place. But not always, not over everything, in a world where there were great dangers and sur-
prises at every turn, from dawn to dusk. Love did not lose
its meaning or restoring power even when death became a
certainty. And when you walked in death's shadow ordinary conventions could lose most, if not quite all, of their
meaning.

Would it be like that with—Joan stopped, refusing for
a moment to dwell on another possibility that had crept,
unbidden, into her mind. But only for a moment. There
was no reason for her to conceal from herself what she
knew to be true. Only some quaint, residually puritanical
part of herself had kept her from sleeping in Dorman's
arms during the days of tormenting uncertainty they had
spent alone in the deep jungle. But in this terrifying world
of snow and ice—

A few days longer, perhaps, not more. There had been

no real excuse for what had not happened so far between them—except that she had never liked to be rushed and Dorman had respected that peculiarity in her, despite the fact that it made her quite unlike a great many women, and probably unlike the ones she was quite sure must have set out for him in the past.

Joan sat up abruptly, a chill apprehension making her strain her ears in the semi-darkness. What she heard drove every previous thought from her mind and sent a coldness darting up her spine.

There *were* movements just outside the hut—distinct, unmistakable. A crunching sound had come to her ears, followed by what sounded like harsh breathing.

On two or three previous occasions in her life Joan had been confronted with two choices—one wholly reasonable, that made sense and the other dangerous and foolish. And there had seemed to be something, deep in her nature, that had turned the dangerous choice into a kind of challenge, blinding her to all caution.

Awakening Dorman instantly was what nine women out of ten would have done—no, ninety-nine out of a hundred. But just the knowledge that her security was being threatened made her determined to investigate the threat for herself.

After all, there would be very little risk, she told herself, in creeping stealthily to the high, oblong opening that Ames had cut in the ice to serve as a doorway, and staring out into the night. She would have to be careful, of course, to remain well inside the opening, merely peering cautiously around its right-hand edge, where the wall ended and there was a hazy glimmering several feet wide.

She did not think it would be difficult to do that, to just let her head emerge into the night for an instant, her eyes trained on the snow directly in front of the hut, from where the crunching sound seemed to be coming.

Some trick of the semi-darkness, with its contrasting shadows, pale gray and inky black, made Dorman's sleeping form seem larger than it actually was. Although he was not, like Ames, a near-giant, he had a lean and powerful body and there was not an ounce of excess flesh on him.

As Joan moved past him a very feminine thought

flashed across her mind. She and Tlacha were more fortunate than a great many women exposed to constant danger. They were both guarded by good men to have around in an emergency. Even when you did a stupid thing and let yourself forget that love was a two-way street it was reassuring to know that.

It was going against something that was basic to a love relationship to deny a man who would be eager to leap to your defense an opportunity to do so. She was cheating the sleeping man as well as herself by letting him slumber on. But it was too late now for her to regret her betrayal in that respect. She had moved so swiftly that she was already at the entrance of the hut staring out, her palm resting on the edge of the ice block that had been partly cut away to produce the oblong opening.

At first she saw only a white expanse of snow and ice broken up into a checkerboard pattern of light and shadow. It was not a moonless night. But the moon had passed behind some medium-dense clouds directly overhead, and the light that filtered down was the opposite of bright.

There was a slight glare, however, for the light was shining on millions of ice crystals that glittered like diamond dust as they swirled about in a steadily blowing wind. The white expanse kept shifting about as she stared at it, now narrowing to expose an outer fringe of bare, projecting rock and then widening out again.

The footprints did not stand out very clearly and it was not until her eyes had become adjusted to the glare that she recogized them for what they were—five-toed prints of startling size that could not possibly have been made by a beast walking upright.

They had to be human footprints, because every part of the indentations, including the tapering soles, bore an exact resemblance to the prints a barefooted man would have made if he had been stridng about on a surface of wet clay. The fact that the surface was of snow did not diminish their sharpness at all, even though it had taken her a little longer to make them out because of the glare and the smaller indentations which the wind was making in the constantly shifting whiteness.

It did not strain Joan's credulity to believe that there might be a few men of ordinary stature with feet almost fifteen inches in length. But the possibility did nothing to decrease the alarm she experienced when she measured the prints with her eyes.

Some instinct warned her that she was in more danger than she had thought, that even that brief moment of cautious staring had exposed her to a risk that she had not taken seriously enough.

She had almost persuaded herself, before starting across the hut, that the crunching sound had been made by some animal moving about over the snow. Even, perhaps, that it had been caused by the collapse of an overhanging snowbank, in a sudden, unusually strong gust of wind. There were other things that could have caused it. But she had not wanted to believe that what she had heard had been the crunch of human feet moving about in the night over a blanket of snow and ice.

Naked feet. A giant's feet? What kind of man would walk with naked feet on a frozen plain? Surely a stone age barbarian would have fashioned for himself some kind of protective footgear.

Just the thought of a human being that primitive, with soles so inured against the cold, was frightening enough. But what alarmed her still more was the likelihood that if she had been looking out of the hut with her eyes on his footprints he could hardly have remained unaware that his presence had become known to her.

And what if he was now looking at her—crouching in the shadows where the constantly shifting expanse of snow merged with the rocks that the wind had laid bare and watching her with a savage cunning in his eyes?

She had made the mistake of venturing too far into the light, of letting more than her face appear in the opening. She was quick to realize that and quick to take an unsteady step backwards. But her retreat from danger wasn't quick enough.

Something firm and unyielding went around her waist and she was pulled, with a sharp and sudden jerk, right out of the hut into the snow.

She started to scream, but something just as firm

clamped itself over her mouth and smothered the scream before it could leave her throat.

She felt herself being lifted up and began to struggle furiously. She twisted violently about, beating with her fists on what felt like a board covered with fur, but knowing instantly that it was a powerful man's hairy chest against which she was being crushed.

Before she could get a glimpse of his face he was carrying her relentlessly over the snow, still keeping a tight grip on her waist but using his other hand to smother her screams in a different way now. He had removed the hand from her mouth and was keeping her face pressed against his chest by entwining his fingers in her hair, and thrusting her head forward and downward until her nose and mouth felt crushed. Against the iron-ridged muscles of his rib cage her mouth could neither open nor close, and she felt herself to be in danger of smothering to death.

She stopped struggling, realizing how useless resistance would be, and it was not until she had been carried a considerable distance from the hut that his grip on her waist relaxed a little and he allowed her to raise her head.

For an instant her only concern was to draw the cold air deep into her bursting lungs. Each breath was followed by a sharp stab of pain, and if another full minute had gone by she was sure that there would have been no need for her to breath at all.

She was sure as well that it was not pity that had made him draw back from smothering her to death. But when she raised her eyes and saw the cruel, thin-lipped face that was staring down at her, the fact that he had spared her at all—for any reason—was hard to understand.

How could the owner of such a face, with his every primitive instinct aroused to fever pitch by an act of violence, be capable of stopping short, of exercising restraint? Could a jungle beast, similarly aroused, its blood lust out of control, turn abruptly and walk away from some small animal of the jungle that it had been on the verge of killing.

Oh, God, no! Joan thought, a little wildly. And yet she was not being smothered again. Instead the shaggy-browed, savage-looking giant—he was barely a giant, despite the largeness of his naked feet—was now slowly, almost concernedly, setting her down on the snow.

He set her down and then, the instant she was on her feet, stood back from her and looked at her with his narrowed, darkly gleaming eyes passing with a chilling kind of deliberation from her ankles to the tousled hair he had just released.

But was it so chilling, she wondered wildly. Was he not merely studying her with the simple, natural curiosity of a man from another age, who had never before set eyes on a woman like herself?

There was something about him that did not seem savage, that made her feel that he was not as brutal as he looked.

And just how brutal did he look, if you made allowances for the fact that his features were of a more primitive cast that museum reconstructions of paleolithic man might have led twentieth-century man to expect, if he had been able to travel back into the past and look at a glacial age barbarian in the flesh?

His hair was matted and straggly, his face encrusted with dirt and he did have a cruel slant to his lips. But even that could be deceptive, could mean very little in itself. Cruelty could take many forms, and sometimes a man of kindly instincts could have a cruel streak in his nature, and could become unduly harsh when he was confronted with something hateful and his anger got out of control.

Somehow Joan did not feel that she was hateful in the huge man's sight. The set of his lips could have been a kind of tropism, over which he had no actual control.

Suddenly he did a surprising thing. He turned and pointed toward the wide expanse of snow and ice directly ahead of them. The moon had now come out from behind a cloud and the plain was bathed in a silvery radiance. But it seemed to shine even more brightly on the tall barbarian's massive shoulders, which were crisscrossed by thin, interlacing strips of fur.

Without uttering a word he started off across the snow. When he had gone ten or twelve paces, he turned abruptly and gestured to Joan to fall in behind him. She obeyed, knowing that she had no choice.

CHAPTER TEN

A man may awaken from a deep sleep and discover that the world has not changed at all and rejoice, because he would not have wanted it to change. Or, if he has fallen asleep feeling wretched, wanting to die, he may curse the sun and moon and stars on finding there has been no improvement in his lot and that another dreary day has dawned.

No man could have wanted the world to change more than Dorman did—to change back from a frozen waste to —yes, even the steaming tropical jungles of central Mexico. But his first impulse, on opening his eyes, was to rejoice.

The world could hardly have changed more, or the shadows taken on an uglier look. But one part of it had not changed and that part had become, in a sense, almost the whole of his life.

It was called "Joan", and there were hills and rivers and valleys in the depths of it, sunlit vistas serene and golden, and still lakes gleaming in the moonlight, and far in the distance a mountain village where there was singing and dancing from dawn to dusk.

He had awakened in a cramped position, with one arm bent under him and sustaining so much of his weight that it had gone to sleep. He lifted it, shook it, tried to flex his fingers and couldn't. He massaged it with his free hand, and gradually life and strength crept back into it.

The rest of him was certainly quite different from the arm, very much alive, not in the least in the need of resuscitation, despite the fact that even two skins had failed to keep him as warm as he had hoped they would and the cold had crept into his bones.

But there was still Joan—Joan right beside him or close to him—and he had a sudden impulse to spring to his feet and surprise her by bending down and taking her in his arms. He wanted to say: "Hey, little lazybones. You've

85

overslept here just as you did once or twice in the jungle, when we had a thousand eyes watching us."

He got to his feet without even looking toward her, because there are impulses which afford more delight when they are postponed, when a little time is allowed to elapse between the thought and the deed.

Then, abruptly he swung about and looked down—she wasn't there. His eyes swept the hut quickly.

The alarm that came upon him started as a chill foreboding, but it quickly turned into something much worse that caused the blood to rush to his temples and made him feel that his brain was about to explode.

He was at the entrance of the hut, staring out, before the thought of awakening Ames and Tlacha could more than flash across his mind. He stared down at the ground and for a moment saw only an unbroken expanse of snow, tarnished, here and there, by murky gleams of dawnlight.

Then he saw the footprints—a single pair of prints leading toward a gray, projecting boulder about thirty feet from where he was standing.

It was impossible for him to picture the man who had left such enormous impressions in the snow as being less of a giant than Ames and certainly difficult not to think of him as being a great deal taller in stature.

There were no small prints in the vicinity of the large ones or anywhere on the level expanse of snow—no signs at all of a struggle.

Dorman turned and went back into the hut. He crossed to where Ames and Tlacha were sleeping and shook them awake—first Ames and then Tlacha without saying a word.

It would be better, he felt, if he did not try to speak for a moment. His voice would only come in a strangled sob and add to Ames' dazed bewilderment at being awakened so abruptly.

Big men always seemed to have a tendency to wake up slowly, to take longer to blink sleep from their eyelids than men of ordinary size. Dorman had noticed that on several occasions in the past. But it made him angry to think that Ames' slowness in waking up might delay his getting her back again and he began to thump him on the shoulder with fierce impatience, for Tlacha was already awake and staring at him with frightened, questioning eyes.

"What is it?" she asked. Then, almost instantly, "Where's Joan? Has something happened to Joan?"

"She's gone," Dorman managed to get out. "When I woke up—she wasn't here. There are footprints in the snow outside."

"Footprints? Oh, no! The ax. He must have come back."

Ames was coming awake now, struggling to a sitting position. He seemed to have heard what Dorman had said— or perhaps only what Tlacha had said—for his first words were, "The ax! It was stolen, all right—it was stolen. He's come back, you say? I was afraid he would—"

"He's come back and carried Joan off!" Dorman heard himself saying. "There are footprints in the snow!"

Ames reached out and gripped Dorman's arm. "God, that's bad. Christ. But we'll find them, don't worry David. We'll take the gun and the bow. Tlacha, get the arrows."

"It's the footprints I'm worried about," Dorman said. "If snow has fallen in the night, and they only go a short distance—"

"We'll do what we can," Ames said, standing now, trying to shake the last bit of sleep off. "Try to stay steady. We'll do what we can—"

"It's good enough for me," Dorman said. "But we haven't much time to lose. I don't know when she was carried off. I just woke up and found her gone."

Fully awake now, Ames turned to Dorman. "You're sure she was carried off? Perhaps she got restless and went outside for a while—before the man with the prints even appeared—"

"No, I don't think so; there was only one set of footprints."

Ames reached out and took firm hold of Tlacha's wrist. But his big hand seemed to envelop almost her entire arm.

"You're not going with us," he said. "You'll be in danger here—entirely alone. But you'll be in a great deal more danger if you accompany us."

"Why don't you stay here with Tlacha and let me go alone," Dorman said. "I wasn't thinking—"

Ames shook his head. "You're going to need help," he said. "I made the bow and it's a supple weapon for me now. And we might just need it."

"Then you'd better let Tlacha keep the gun."

"No!" Tlacha said. "You'll need both weapons. Harvey has left me alone before—many times. He had to, or we would have had no food."

Ames turned and went into a shadowed corner of the hut. He bent and picked up a great bow which gleamed in the firelight. He returned to where Dorman and Tlacha were standing with the bow slung over his shoulder.

"We'd better get started," he said.

Suddenly he turned and took Tlacha into his arms, crushing her to him. "We'll be back," he whispered as he held her close. He tried to speak again, but stopped himself.

Then he was passing with Dorman at his side through the entrance of the hut and out onto the frozen plain.

CHAPTER ELEVEN

It was a world of stillness, in which everything seemed to be in motion. It was not a paradox which could be easily explained or resolved, for all of the movements were subtle, mysterious, hidden.

Gazing out across that desolate expanse of snow and ice it was impossible for Dorman to detect the slightest movement, beyond the slight flurries of snow raised by the constantly blowing wind. Yet out of the corners of his eyes he caught glimpses of what appeared to be evanescent shapes of darkness, darting in and out of the shadows that clustered thickly about the projecting ledges of rock which were scattered across the plain at intervals, their summits gilded by the dawn light.

If he swung about to catch their movement, the shapes managed instantly to vanish. But the moment he plodded on again they returned, and it was very hard to ignore the gnawing feeling that both he and Ames were, in some wholly incomprehensible way, being intensely scrutinized from a distance, and every stage of their progress noted.

Their confidence that Joan could and would be found, that they would somehow succeed in overcoming all obstacles had begun to waver just a little when the vastness of the plain and the number of rock structures that could have provided concealment for the man who had carried her off was brought forcibly home to them.

But suddenly all of their confidence came back. Not only were the huge footprints still clearly visible, but they were accompanied now by much smaller ones.

Not exactly accompanied, perhaps, for Joan's prints—they had no doubt at all that it was Joan who had left the small sandal marks in the snow—trailed those of the giant - by twenty-five or thirty feet.

They had begun a short distance from the hut and were continuing on now without a break.

Just the fact that Joan was not walking by the giant's

side made Dorman come to an abrupt halt the instant he realized what that could have meant.

"He's not dragging her ruthlessly along," he said, gripping Ames' arm. "He's letting her walk behind him. She couldn't be making an effort to escape. If she ran a short distance and he went after her and dragged her back the snow would be all torn up in spots."

"I'd say she's badly frightened and doing the wise thing," Ames said. "The worst thing she could do would be to enrage the brute by struggling with him."

"Brute? Do we have to think that? Are all barbarians monsters?"

"You're right in one way, of course," Ames said. "But you've got to be realistic about it as well. What seems traditionally right, tribally sanctioned to a Stone Age primitive could seem plenty brutal to us."

"But individuals differ."

"I hope you're right," Ames said.

They continued on in tight-lipped silence, but had put the hut no more than another half mile behind them when Dorman came to a halt again.

"I'm pretty sure that someone is following us," he said. "I just looked back and there was a shadow on the snow —a kind of darting shadow that disappeared behind that long ridge of rock we passed a moment ago."

He turned quickly, before Ames could protest—as he had done once before—that they would be surrounded, outnumbered and hopelessly at the mercy of a thousand and one illusionary pursuers—if they made the mistake of letting themselves believe that shadows could have a mysterious life of their own.

Dorman had not expected Ames to protest very strenuously but was more than a little surprised when he said, "I saw it too. I guess we'd better go back and have a look."

They started back toward the rock ridge, walking as fast as they could without stumbling or sliding on the frozen plain.

"If you want to catch a shadow you've got to put everything that makes sense out of your mind," Ames said. "If you're in just the right lunatic state, maybe it can be done. But we'd better not count on it."

"Shadows are cast by something, as a rule," Dorman said.

"All right, we'll know in a moment."

The stone ridge had a jagged summit and projected about six feet above the plain. The snow was quite deep at its base and the two plodding men sank into it almost up to their knees before they reached the other side, where it was banked less high.

Half way down the length of the ridge a shadowy form was crouching—but it wasn't a shadow. It leapt up just as Dorman and Ames came into view and turned into a tiny woman. Despite its tininess Dorman thought for an instant that it was Joan, so constantly present had she been in his thoughts.

But only Tlacha could have been that tiny, and the illusion vanished in a matter of seconds. Ames helped to shatter it by shouting her name and staring at her in angry disbelief as she seemed almost to fly into his arms.

He clasped and held her for a moment, then set her down, frowning.

"I might have known!" he flung at her. "If you were determined to come—why didn't you tell me? I pleaded with you not to make it difficult for me. You knew how hard it was for me to—"

She silenced him by standing on tiptoe and placing two of her fingers across his mouth.

"You're glad I'm here," she said. "Deep down—you're glad. I had to wait, of course—until you were too far from the hut to turn back."

She turned quickly and looked at Dorman and there was something in her expression that made him feel that it was his forgiveness that she was less sure of.

"I've delayed you," she said. "Every minute is precious and I made you turn back and search for me. I intended simply to join you, but you must have seen me moving back and forth between the rocks."

"It's all right," Dorman said. "We haven't lost more than five minutes. Ten at most. We may be following

Joan's footprints an hour from now, or even longer. We don't know how far away she may be by now."

"Joan's footprints?" Tlacha looked startled. "I saw only the huge ones."

"Joan's began a short distance from the hut," Dorman explained. "She must have been lifted up and carried. There were no signs of a struggle, though—anywhere along the trail we've been following."

"Finding Joan's footprints must have been a great relief to you."

"It was, in a way," Dorman said. "It eliminates the possibility that—well, it proves at least that she's still able to walk without assistance. But for a while I kept remembering what Harvey said before we left the hut—she might have gotten up and gone outside before the intruder arrived. It was a slim reed to cling to, but if you're desperate enough you'll magnify the importance of a possibility like that. Finding her footprints running in a straight line with the huge ones crumpled that reed up."

"Tlacha, just how happy does it make you to know that you've put an added burden on my shoulders?" Ames asked. "You know what would happen to me if anything happened to you."

"You will soon forgive me," Tlacha said. "You think you know yourself, but I am the only one who understands you."

"Maybe you're right," Ames said. "I don't know too much about myself—but I do know that I can be a very hard-headed, down-to-earth kind of man when there's something that has to be done. Right now that means finding Joan—helping David find her before she's harmed in any way. And you've made it more difficult for me. Now I have to worry about your safety as well."

"Do you want me to go back?"

"Yes, I'd like that. But I know damned well that you won't. So we'll all have to go on together. I can't imagine any situation in which a woman would be more of a handicap."

Five minutes later they were following the footprints again, Tlacha walking at Ames' side and Dorman moving on a few feet ahead.

Dorman knew that although Ames was still pretending to be angry, he was secretly glad that Tlacha had joined them. It was natural enough and he would have felt the same way if Joan had come running out to join him on some other dangerous undertaking. It was just as natural, certainly, to want to spare someone you loved all exposure to danger. But love had its selfish side, and when you balanced the two, the scales fell about even.

They had walked on for close to another mile before they saw any change in the frozen plain. There was something in the distance that did not look like a rock structure or a high snowbank, but it was impossible for them to determine what it was until they were within a hundred feet of it.

CHAPTER TWELVE

It was a slain animal. It lay sprawled out across the plain with its four short legs standing straight up from its furry body—and projecting from it were the dark shafts of three arrows.

The closer they came to it the more sure they were that it was quite dead, for its body was rigid and there was a wide circle of congealed blood on the ice and snow surrounding it.

Huge as it was, it was not as gigantic as the beast in the Gulf or the one which Dorman and Ames had encountered. It looked like an enormous, white-furred beaver, with its long, sharp teeth bared in a death grimace.

Tlacha clung tightly to Ames' arm as they approached it, her eyes wide with wonder.

"None of the beasts you killed were one-tenth as large as that," she breathed. "It would have supplied us with fresh meat for a month."

"It seems to belong to the rodent family," Dorman said. "But just what species of animal it is—well, that doesn't seem too important right now. Something else seems more vital at the moment."

He turned to Ames as he spoke, his eyes questioning.

Ames nodded. "You mean—the arrows—"

"There are barbarian huntsmen in the vicinity," Dorman said. "We couldn't have more conclusive proof of it."

"I'm not so sure," Ames said. "They could be nomad hunters—far away by now."

"But would they just slay the beast and depart, with no intention of returning for it? Unless, of course, it attacked them and they slew it to protect themselves—"

"It would be a mistake to stay here and find out," Ames said. "There could be a large number of barbarian hunters roaming about. The chances are slim that the one who slew that beast is the one who carried Joan off."

"It would make no sense at all to stay here when the

footprints can tell us in exactly what direction he was heading," Dorman said. "But I still think there may be a primitive settlement of some kind in the immediate vicinity—a cluster of ice-block huts perhaps."

"Just possibly, if we circled around before going on and made a cautious search for it we'd gain a certain advantage. We'd be less likely to be attacked by surprise, we'd know exactly what kind of odds we'd be facing. But I wouldn't advise it *now*."

It was Tlacha who was the first to discover a new and different set of footprints. It was not surprising that neither Dorman nor Ames had seen them immediately, for the snow around the slain beast had been heavily trampled by the struggle it had put up before crashing to the plain.

It was easy for Dorman to picture the struggle, the great beast arising in embattled fury, and the hunter—or hunters—dwarfed by its immensity, recoiling in terror and sending arrow after arrow speeding toward it. Or had they been cool and undaunted, barbarians clad in the skins of animals just as formidable, skilled of eye and hand, totally sure of themselves?

Tlacha had taken firm hold of Ames' arm and was drawing him a little forward, pointing down at two very clear prints in the trampled snow, very close to the slain beast.

"Harvey, look!" she exclaimed, her voice tremulous. "Those prints are as large as the ones we've been following. A little larger, I think—"

Both Dorman and Ames stared down at the prints for a moment without saying a word.

Then Ames shrugged. "It stands to reason that all the prints we'll find will be about the same size," he said. "Otherwise it would mean that the giant who carried Joan off was some kind of anthropological freak, quite different from other members of his tribe, or whatever you want to call their bond of kinship. There is the possibility, of course, that ordinary-sized men and giants roam this plain side by side, but that seems unlikely. In an age of primitive weapons, a physically giant-like race would have killed off its smaller competitors."

"Or enslaved them," Dorman said. "In that case, we could find some smaller footprints."

Ames was silent for a moment. Then he said: "I don't think so. The remote past was probably quite unlike the way we've pictured it. Look. You see a lot of large footprints scattered about and you immediately start thinking of tribal warfare, the beginnings of slavery, and a complex social organization along with the warfare. I prefer simply to believe that men of huge stature roam these plains, period. They're just big, that's all—and they probably have some pretty ugly customs, from our so-called 'civilized' point of view."

Ames grimaced in self-reproach for the additional discomfort he had brought Dorman. He drew Tlacha away from the footprints close to the beast, and gestured toward the tracks they had been following.

"Time is all-important now," he said. "And we've been wasting far too much of it."

Dorman nodded in tormented agreement, and they were soon moving across the plain again. The footprints stretched out ahead of them without the slightest break. Dorman was somewhat relieved because he had been afraid that they might suddenly vanish, and be replaced by an even longer stretch of untrodden snow.

They had traveled on for what must have been close to another mile when they came across another slain beast.

The second beast was even larger than the first, and there were at least a dozen long-shafted arrows projecting from it. It was elephant-like, and its gigantic tusks were deeply embedded in the ice above its grotesquely distorted, wool-coated body. A red stain had spread out from the tusks over the ice, but it was the tremendous mountain of flesh that towered above the tusks that brought Ames and Dorman to an abrupt halt and made Tlacha cry out in stunned disbelief.

Yet when Ames finally spoke, his voice was as calm as it had been when a monster quite different and infinitely more terrifying had gone careening away from the buckling gun in Dorman's hand.

"It's a woolly mammoth," he said. "We've got a time-clock now. It's the first indication we've had that this must be the last glacial age, not an earlier one. An age of mammals, large ones—and pleistocene man."

Dorman was on the verge of crying out, as he had done once before, because it outraged something basic to his nature, *How can you stay so calm!*

Then he remembered what Ames had said, that he was a calm man only externally, and forced himself to feel contrite.

"Under ordinary circumstances I'd like to get a closer look at it," Ames went on, not quite as calmly. "I'd like to spend a week here, just looking up at it first, just standing quietly and letting the strangeness and wonder—the poetry of it—take firm hold of me. A woolly mammoth! After that I'd start taking measurements and waiting for the expeditions to arrive."

Dorman had to fight against reminding him that woolly mammoths had been found in Siberia quite often—their carcasses encased in the frozen soil, even the meat so well preserved that it could be consumed in perfect safety. But the living beast—or one just slain—yes, it was different. Again he felt ashamed of his quick judgments.

Then his concern for Joan's safety came rushing back and nothing else seemed of the slightest importance to him.

It required no urging on his part, however, to start Ames and Tlacha moving on again. Ames' face was now set in grim lines, as if the time they had lost, despite its brevity, had begun to weigh more heavily on him. He not only shared Dorman's concern for Joan's safety, but was worried about what effect the strain and uncertainty might have on his friend if nothing arose to give them some grounds for hope.

The third beast was lying just beyond a slight rise in the plain which had concealed it from view until they were almost upon it.

It was an enormous, snow-white boar. Its tusks were almost as long as those of the woolly mammoth, and it was only slightly smaller in size. There were eight arrows projecting from it, one deeply buried in its neck. It lay on its side on the plain, and had evidently put up a tremendous struggle, for the snow around it had been tossed high on both sides of it, exposing a wide expanse of naked earth which gleamed like burnished copper in the dawnlight.

The footprints circled closer to it than they had to the other two beasts and Ames halted for a moment before descending the far side of the slope, his hand raised in a warning gesture.

"Stay back," he said. "There's something—I'm not sure, but I could have sworn its flanks moved a little, as if it might still be alive. We shouldn't have gone as close to that beaver-like animal as we did. We'd better not repeat the mistake."

"I don't see how it could possibly be alive, "Tlacha said. "Eight arrows—and one of them in its neck."

"Let's not take a chance," Dorman said, quickly. "Harvey's right. We can return to the footprints again easily enough, if we stay at least a hundred feet from it until it's a considerable distance behind us."

"We'd better not even descend the slope at this point," Ames said. "That would also bring us too close. Wait—"

He gestured along the top of the slope. "Just walk about seventy feet," he said. "That should be far enough. We can widen the distance a little more when we're on level ground again."

A moment later they were descending at what had seemed like a safe distance. But the instant they were at the bottom of the slope and saw that the boar had begun to stir they realized that they had made a mistake.

A convulsive shudder passed over it, and before they could swing about and start back up the slope again it had heaved itself to its feet and was rushing straight toward them, its red-rimmed eyes gleaming in the dawnlight and its blood-streaked flanks moving in and out.

So swift was its pain-maddened charge that it was less than thirty feet from the slope before Ames could free his great bow from the thin strip of furskin that encircled his shoulder, snatch an arrow from the loose-hanging quiver at his waist, notch it into the bowstring, draw the bowstring back, and take careful aim.

Barely ten feet separated the charging boar from the slope when the arrow found its mark, burying itself between the enraged beast's flesh-embedded eyes, and bringing it to a shuddering halt.

Both of its front legs collapsed, and it crashed forward in a headlong sprawl that carried it three feet further through the snow. It took a long time to die, seeming to grow more monstrous and misshapen as its life ebbed away. The shape that remained on the frozen plain when the last, convulsive spasm had passed looked more like some white-furred animal of indeterminate shape with crushed bones than it did a wild boar.

Ames returned the great bow to his shoulder, and tightened the strip of furskin to make sure that it would be held firmly in place. He looked with concern at Tlacha, who seemed to be having great difficulty in regaining control of herself. She was swaying a little, but when Ames moved forward to steady her, she waved him aside.

"No—we must keep on," she said, her voice emotion-choked. "Just as if this hadn't happened. We mustn't stop now, not even to tell ourselves how lucky we are to be alive."

Dorman, who hadn't moved at all, reached out and let his hand rest for a moment on the tiny woman's shoulder. He gave it a gentle squeeze, knowing that she would not misunderstand, would know that he was thanking her for her courage and concern.

There was no need now to remain at a distance from the slain beast when they continued on. They returned to where the footprints stretched out across the snow in an unbroken double line.

There was no evidence that Joan's steps had faltered at any time in what had now turned into quite a long journey. For that, at least, Dorman was grateful.

How many miles, he wondered, had they traveled after the hut had dwindled and vanished in the blanketing whiteness? Four or five, surely—perhaps more.

They plodded on in silence now, still shaken by what they had seen. Death in violent form had clearly come to the plain, and although animals slain by huntsmen would not be a chilling sight in the world from which they had come, it was quite different here. Not only the size of the animals but the savage nature of the age, where such beasts, red in tooth and claw, preyed on one another and on man as well, struck a chill to Dorman's heart.

Did it not mean that the huntsmen as well had learned from childhood to walk in death's shadow with an instant readiness to kill—the great beasts certainly and perhaps their fellow tribesmen when disputes arose as to the ownership of a kill?

Could strangers in such a world, speaking an unknown language, peculiar in other ways—outrageously different, in fact—expect mercy at their hands?

The plain had begun to slope slightly upward again when there came to Dorman's ears the far-off beating of drums.

CHAPTER THIRTEEN

Dorman was the first to halt, straining his ears to make sure the incredible sound was not caused by the wind—blowing through some distant rock cavern with echoing walls or swirling the snow about in such a way that it was creating a kind of revolving sounding board.

The sound was very faint at first, but the instant it grew louder he knew that it could only be made by actual drums, beaten rhythmically by human hands. It bore too close a resemblance to the jungle drums he had heard, not only in Mexico, but in every part of the world into which tape recorders had been carried.

He had studied every drumbeat ever heard on Earth in the twentieth century and their remote origins as well and it had been part of the long hours of study he had devoted to gaining a museum assignment in the pre-Columbian field.

Ames had halted now and so had Tlacha.

"Drums," Ames said. "It's—unbelievable. Paleolithic man could never have constructed drums. They were not out of the crude flint stage."

"Couldn't they?" Dorman asked. "How about the arrows they slew those animals with? There's nothing so very complicated about a drum. It's just about the most primitive musical instrument there is."

"But they didn't have music," Ames protested.

"Oh, come off it," Dorman said. "It probably preceded sign language or guttural speech. They had drums, all right, and other sound-producing instruments. I always thought so and I'm sure of it now. You can't expect musical artifacts to have survived for a million years. The crudely chipped flints from the Old Stone Age, so-called, were probably just something the children played around with."

Dorman went on after a pause, "Henley wrote, 'The

101

rhythms aped from nature in the infancy of music.' Those drums are reproducing those rhythms right now."

"Tell me something," Ames said. "How recent are woolly mommoths? I mean—aren't there some geologists who believe the last glacial age wasn't so long ago? And that the men who hunted the mammoth and the mastodon may have been neolithic barbarians?"

"We just don't know for sure," Dorman said. "It depends on what geologic time scale you favor. It's been pushed further and further back in recent years. I would say, at a rough guess, the pleistocene must have been at least a million years ago, although some geologists think it hasn't ended yet. And a million years ago man was, theoretically at least, paleolithic."

"It's hellishly confusing," Ames said. "At least, it has always impressed me that way. A million years could mean the same thing as fifty thousand years, couldn't it— on a different geologic time scale?"

"It could, yes. That's why we don't know really what the men of the last glacial age were like—whether they were stone age savages or neolithic barbarians. And I'm not sure there was ever such a thing as a stone age savage, unless you want to go all the way back to Dawn Man. We don't know how far paleolithic man may have advanced culturally in specialized directions. There are perishable artifacts that couldn't possibly have survived into our age, even if they had been *buried* with men of the Old Stone Age."

The drumbeats were drawing nearer now. They were quite unlike the aboriginal music-making or message-sending sounds that arose in the deep jungles of Africa and South America. They seemed rhythmically simple— simple in a complex way.

Somehow it chilled Dorman.

Tlacha had drawn closer to Ames, and they were both standing now staring at the plain ahead, rigidly attentive, as if they feared that the slightest bodily movement might make their hearing less acute.

The sound had become almost deafening when the wide stretch of plain ahead of them filled with swarming shapes. Their sudden appearance, Dorman knew, had to mean

that there was a deep downward slope in the plain just beyond the next rise, which, though slight, had concealed
what lay beyond.

Now they were swarming over the rise and ceasing to be
just dark shapes silhouetted against the sky. The drum-
beaters seemed to be advancing the fastest, but the others
were moving swiftly enough. There were fifty or sixty of
them and the sunlight glittered on their stone weapons—
some long and slender, shaped like spears, and others
short and hatchet-like, and attached to their wrists by dangling strips of leather. The drums were huge and so were
the men who carried them, their massive fists rising and
falling as if they were hammering out a design in bronze to
accompany the sound with iron-ridged knuckles.

They were not as tall as Dorman had thought they
might be, with only the footsteps to guide him. But none
of them were less than six feet and a half in height, and
most of them were considerably taller.

It was their features which startled him the most. They
were almost Dawn Man primitives—if museum reconstructions could be trusted—and not in the least Cro-
Magnon-like. Nearly as startling was the way they were
clad. A few of them were nine-tenths naked, with no more
than a thin furskin encircling their loins. Others wore
patches and shreds of fur that could have afforded them
little protection from the cold, for the scanty garments left
most of their shoulders exposed, and their lower limbs
completely bare.

Their hardihood in defying the cold made Dorman fear,
as they narrowed the distance which separated them from
Ames—who for some unaccountable reason was walking
straight toward them across the plain—that they might be
equally hardy in other, less *self*-punishing ways.

Ames was within ten feet of the drummers, who were
advancing in double file, when he came to an abrupt halt
and raised his arms. Dorman suddenly realized that Ames
had foolishly allowed himself to think that this was a gesture of friendship, primitive in its origin, universal in its
appeal.

It was too late now to shout that he was making a terrible mistake, that the gesture could mean many things, that

there were primitive tribes who preferred to believe it meant defiance, a willingness to engage in a struggle to the death—or the deadliest kind of insult.

Dorman's alarm increased when he saw that all of the drummers had ceased to advance and had stopped beating upon their drums. And at their backs, too, there was a stillness, scarcely a movement on the plain.

Tlacha seemed to share his alarm, for there was even more fear in her eyes now than when she had first caught sight of the drummers and the men with stone weapons who had come swarming down over the rise at almost the same moment.

It happened so suddenly that for an instant Dorman could not believe that what he had feared was actually taking place. One of the tallest of the warriors—the drums had made it impossible for him not to think of them as warriors as well as primitive hunters—strode past the drummers and stood facing Ames with a look of smouldering rage in his eyes. A stone hatchet dangled from an arm that was sharply bent at the elbow and that terminated in a tightly clenched fist.

He was close to seven feet tall and bore himself with the look of a leader. Suddenly his arm shot out, hatchet and all, and struck Ames a savage blow on the head.

The hatchet went swinging past Ames' skull, but the fist landed squarely on the right side of his head and dropped him to the snow.

Dorman shook off the inertia which had come upon him for an instant, and started across the snow toward where Ames was lying, crumpled up and unmoving. Tlacha gripped him fiercely by the arm.

"No, wait!" she pleaded. "You will only get yourself killed and he would not want that. Remember what he said—Joan was wise not to struggle. You can do more to save him by waiting."

Her voice broke for an instant, then went on with an even wilder insistence. "He is beginning to move. Let him get up by himself. He will know what to do. We must not enrage them further."

Dorman would have ignored her advice, feeling that he

could do more than a man dazed by so savage a blow to
pacify the tall warrior, if Ames had gotten to his feet more
slowly. But Ames had not remained for more than a few
seconds sprawled out on the plain and now he was gesturing to Dorman as he arose, and echoing Tlacha's words.

"Stay back—stay where you are!" he shouted, "We've
got to convince them we're not dangerous!"

It flashed across Dorman's mind that there was very little likelihood the tall warrior had thought of Ames in that
way, with so many men at his back, and defenseless as
Ames had been. Clearly it was the gesture which Ames
had made that had enraged him. But Ames was not as un-
forewarned now, and that, at least, made his shouted
words seem worth heeding. Ames had armed himself in
the only way that mattered, with a quickly arrived at,
cool-headed realization that the giant facing him had to be
mollified in some way.

Otherwise—death, swift and unmerciful, was certain to
ensue and Tlacha would not be spared.

Dorman's admiration and respect for Ames increased
when he saw how the big man was going about it. He was
shaking his head, spreading his arms in a gesture of de-
fenselessness, calling the tall warrior's attention to the fact
that he was carrying no weapons other than the bow
strapped to his back by partially removing both his outer
and his inner skins. Dorman caught a flash of metal and
knew that the pistol had come into view. But it seemed
unlikely that the tall warrior would think of that as a
weapon.

Or would he? Puzzled by it he certainly would be, and
if he got the idea it was some kind of death-dealing thun-
der stick—

Dorman's uncertainty changed to relief when he saw
that the tall warrior was allowing Ames to let the outer skin
fall back over the holstered weapon strapped to his waist
without demanding that he be allowed to examine the gun.

Perhaps he feared to touch it but had persuaded himself
that if it were truly dangerous Ames would not .have allowed him to see it. It was impossible to know how a
mechanical contrivance—or any metal object—would be

interpreted in a stone-age culture by a mind totally incapable of thinking of metal in other than its natural state.

Ames was displaying his helplessness in a wholly calm and courageous way, letting the warrior see that he was bowing to circumstance only because he had no choice. He was meeting the warrior's gaze with no outward display of fear, and although, being human, he could hardly have been untouched by fear, few men could have summoned quite so much composure to their aid.

Quite possibly there were men who loved life but did not really fear death at all. It could not be absolutely ruled out, but somehow Dorman did not think that Ames was such a man. He had never met and talked with such a man and his own inclinations could hardly have been said to tend in that direction. Facing death with reasonable resolution and not caring when your last breath came were two quite different things. The tall warrior had walked a few steps away from Ames now and was pacing back and forth in front of him. He kept his eyes trained on him for the most part, but darted occasional glances toward Dorman and Tlacha, as if to make sure they would not attempt to flee.

It may or may not have been little different from the pacing of a twentieth century man deep in thought, not quite able to make up his mind about some vexing problem. But it became more curious, more difficult to explain, when the tall warrior stopped pacing in a straight line, and began slowly to encircle Ames, not once, but a half-dozen times, still keeping his eyes fastened on him.

Could it mean, Dorman wondered a little wildly, that the tall warrior was performing some kind of magical rite —intended, perhaps, to drive suspected evil spirits from the body of the stranger? It was a common enough practice among the Indian tribes of the Amazon Basin, and elsewhere, but it seemed hard to reconcile it with the tall warrior's previous behavior. If he had feared that Ames was possessed by demons, would he have risked felling him with a blow before attempting to drive them forth? To the primitive mind there would be no surer way of enabling evil spirits to leave the body of one man and rush into

that of another than by resorting to such an acto of violence.

Dorman suddenly decided that the tall warrior was
merely encircling Ames to observe him more cautiously
from all sides, to make sure that he was not making a mistake in letting the stone hatchet dangle unused from his
arm.

On the plain there was a stirring now, a growing restlessness, and it was evident that even a tribal leader could
arouse impatience and mistrust if he took too long to
make up his mind.

If Ames' gesture of friendship had been misunderstood,
there was no mistaking the intent behind the gesture which
the tall warrior made when he stopped pacing in a circle
around Ames.

He simply raised his arm and pointed directly at Dorman and Tlacha, his bony forefinger stabbing at the air.
Instantly four hatchet-armed warriors, only a little less tall
than their leader, detached themselves from the restless
group surrounding them and crossed to where Dorman
and Tlacha were standing.

There was a moment of almost unbearable uncertainty
when Dorman's heart stood still and then began to pound
furiously in his chest. There began to grow in him the
strange feeling that in some quite terrible way, a sharp
stone blade had begun to split open his head, was passing
down through his skull, dividing his brain in half.

Then he was stumbling forward, with something that
could have been a human fist, but was as hard as a rock
pressing into the small of his back. He knew then that his
brain was safe, that nothing had happened to it, for the
sunlight was still bright on the snow ahead of him and Tlacha was stumbling along at his side.

He raised his eyes and saw Ames then, waiting for them
to join him, nodding in quiet reassurance. And after that
he became for a moment a little confused again and it was
hard for him to realize that they were all moving together
across the plain in the direction from which the barbarian
warriors had come.

The drums had started up again, and three of the drummers had moved on ahead of them. At least that kept

them from feeling that they were being forced to head a
procession without having the least idea just how long
their lives would be spared, or what moving in the wrong
direction might lead to.

CHAPTER FOURTEEN

The plain had not changed and yet the desolation seemed to have taken on a more ominous aspect, as if beyond every slope there were dark shapes waiting to leap up and join the advancing warriors, swelling their ranks with ghostly presences from the buried past of the earth.

Dorman was kept moving so rapidly, by continuous proddings in the small of his back or between his shoulder blades by what he was convinced was sometimes a hard-knuckled fist and sometimes the blunt end of a stone hatchet, that he had little opportunity to talk to Ames. And the few words he managed to exchange with him were the opposite of reassuring.

Although Ames had regained his customary outward calmness—it had never been more than slightly shaken—he made no attempt to conceal from Dorman how concerned he had become about Tlacha.

"I've no idea what may be passing through their minds," he said. "When that tall Number One Man got through making up his mind about me I tried to put on the best act I could. Tlacha looked about ready to collapse—and you didn't look too good yourself. I tried to make her believe that I was completely reassured, that everything was going to be all right. But I don't really think I succeeded in overcoming their hostility."

"But if you hadn't—wouldn't that glary-eyed savage have knocked you down again? Or gone at you with his hatchet?"

"Perhaps not," Ames said. "I've a feeling we're more valuable to them alive than dead, that he simply lost his head for a moment. He misunderstood my gesture of friendship, apparently."

"I could have told you that," Dorman said. "Consult an archeologist before you do anything that rash again."

"That's water over the dam now," Ames said. "We

haven't the least idea where they're taking us, or what's in store for us. I don't like any part of it."

He glanced back at Tlacha as he spoke, his face set in tight lines. She was stumbling on a few feet behind them, looking tinier than she had ever looked before, between the two tall barbarian warriors who were advancing on opposite sides of her.

"You said—consult an archeologist," Ames went on grimly. "We could use the advice of an anthropologist as well as an ethnologist and a dozen or more highly knowledgeable experts in related fields—including a sociologist with some first-hand knowledge of what the social structure was like in the last glacial age. A good guesser, at the very least. I've never been particularly good at guessing games."

Before Dorman could say anything in reply he was prodded forward again and the next time Ames came abreast of him there was such an anguished look in his friend's eyes that he thought it best to say nothing at all.

They continued on for at least two, possibly three more miles over the frozen plain. But none of the barbarian warriors seemed to be growing even slightly weary and the drums kept up a continuous, rhythmic throbbing.

Then, all at once the plain began to rise at an unusually sharp angle and the merciless prodding at Dorman's back grew so relentless that he was forced to move twice as rapidly as before. The procession passed over the summit of the slope and descended to where the plain was level again with a thunderous beating of drums echoing in Dorman's ears and almost deafening him. Then, abruptly, it came to a halt.

Ahead of them there loomed a high-walled, completely circular structure of ice, not unlike an amphitheater, and although Dorman could not tell from where the procession had halted whether or not it was open to the sky, he had the feeling that it was.

Beside it was a smaller structure, also circular, with a large doorway cut in the ice similar to the one Ames had made with an ax in the ice-block hut—to make it easier for Joan to get up in the night and be seized and carried off? How much better it would have been if the hut had possessed no doorway at all, if Ames had invited them all inside, and straightway demolished it; if he had lighted a fire and let the lack of ventilation bring to them a gentle drowsiness followed by the long sleep of death.

Dorman forced himself to put all such thoughts from his mind, and to cling to the ancient truism that—while there was life there was hope. At this moment it didn't seem such a saccharine cliché to him.

Now he was being prodded forward again, toward the two structures. A swift glance backwards made him realize that while the warriors intended to remain for the most part motionless no such privilege would be extended to their three captives. Ames and Tlacha were being forced to walk forward also, accompanied by the four hatchet-armed warriors that had walked on opposite sides of Tlacha during the journey, and directly behind Ames, with the blunt edges of their hatchets administering a constant jabbing.

At a signal from the Number One Man, as Ames had called him, they had detached themselves from the halted procession and were forcing Ames and Tlacha to cross the hundred feet of snow and ice that separated the base of the slope from what appeared to be the ice-age amphitheatre. Dorman was the first to reach the towering, ice-block structure. But before he could look up at it and measure it with his eyes at close range he was prodded forward into the smaller structure adjacent to it.

What happened then took place so rapidly that it became for a moment a wild fantasmagoria of darting lights and shadows, of high-leaping flames and grotesquely bent and capering nightmare shapes. They seemed to be fiendishly intent on grabbing hold of him and hurling him into the flames before he could recover from the spin-numbing blow that had landed in the middle of his back.

He went hurtling forward, throwing out his arms to keep from falling and collided with a stone-hard wall of ice that hurled him just as violently backwards.

Then he was on his knees on a surface of inches-deep snow, turning slowly about with his vision clearing a little. Even before he could see just what it was that had made

him feel that there were taloned hands plucking and tugging at him, he began to realize that he was not being attacked by shapes of darkness intent on dragging him into
the flames.

The voice that accompanied the tugging was not that of
some fiendish monster but a voice that he recognized, and
the tugging itself quickly ceased to be mercilessly unyielding and became clinging and caressing.

But even when his vision became clear again, he could
not see Joan's face in the firelight, because she had twined
her fingers in his hair and was drawing his head down to
kiss him—madly, passionately on the mouth.

Then their lips met and for a long moment remained in
contact and there was a glory and a sweetness in not stopping to draw breath, in not giving a thought to anything
but the way time had ceased to exist and a foreverness had
rushed in to take its place.

They were still locked in the same unending embrace
when Ames and Tlacha came stumbling into the small,
circular ice structure.

CHAPTER FIFTEEN

They were together again. But if the time during which Joan had been absent had seemed long to Ames and Tlacha, to Dorman it had been forever; it was made more unendurable by the way each minute of the separation had increased his steadily mounting uncertainty and a torment that had never been absent from his mind.

They had been talking continuously for close to an hour, for it had taken that long to acquaint Joan with what had happened. Although Joan had not been silent, it was only now that she was helping them to bring together the two parts of what would have otherwise have been a double kind of puzzle, more jagged around the edges that any puzzle had a right to be.

It was as if the puzzle had been floating on a deepening sea of mystery, and they were doing their best to snatch it from the waves before it became completely submerged.

They were sitting by a fire a little larger and burning more steadily than the one which Ames had been compelled to keep replenishing in the ice-hut with brittle twigs. There seemed to be a better updraft at their backs, for they were experiencing no discomfort from the fumes.

All about them the firelight danced on walls of ice which were approximately fifteen feet high, and completely circular. The circumference was large enough to make the interior of the structure about three times as spacious as the one which Ames had built with only a stone ax and his engineering know-how to aid him.

A massive boulder had been rolled by several of the barbarian warriors to block the almost tombstone-shaped opening that had been cut in the ice to serve as a doorway. Quite possibly Ames and Dorman together could have rolled it away, but at the moment they had no desire to attempt it.

It was far more important, Dorman felt—and probably less suicidal—to attempt nothing of the sort until Joan had

113

fallen silent and he could take her into his arms again. If what she had still to tell them made rolling the stone away seem wise, there would be time enough to weigh the risks of doing it immediately against waiting for the fire to die down. The latter would probably take several hours, and make it less of a risk, since with the coming of darkness there would be more of a likelihood that an escape attempt would succeed.

"The three slain beasts you saw," Joan was saying, "were slain in a single day by a newcomer to the tribe. They now consider him the mightiest of hunters, almost a god."

"But how did you find that out?" Ames asked. "They have a guttural kind of language which it would be difficult to understand even if we had a—well, a kind of glacial-age Rosetta stone."

"I saw the newcomer," Joan said. "I saw him—and he spoke to me. I had no trouble at all in understanding every word he said. And you would have had no trouble either, David. He spoke a coastal-district Mexican dialect—half Indian, half Spanish. I'm sure he must be mad—a very dangerous kind of madman—or he would not have grabbed hold of you in the Gulf and carried you with him when the boat capsized."

Dorman stared at her for a moment in stunned disbelief. "You mean, the bearded youth who tried to prevent me from getting to the harpoon gun? That crazed, fanatical—"

Joan nodded. "The light swirled over him too, David. Just as he was trying to climb on the capsized boat. Remember?"

"I'm not likely to forget it," Dorman said. "But somehow it never occurred to me—Oh, my God. So he followed us—"

"Or got here ahead of us," Joan said, nodding. "There doesn't seem to be the slightest doubt of it, since he *is* here —very dangerously here. He not only hates you, David. As soon as he set eyes on me he tried to—well, he gripped me by the shoulders and struck me across the face. I think he would have killed me if one of those—those savages hadn't dragged him away from me. Oh, I shouldn't call them that. The one who carried me here never laid a hand on me, after he set me down, and the one who saved me risked his own life as well. As I told you, after that madman slew the beasts they almost worship him as a god."

Ames seemed to have lost more of his calmness than Dorman would have thought possible, barring some suddenly arising incident threatening Tlacha's life.

"Did he tell the barbarian who carried you off to bring you here?" Ames asked. "I mean—did you talk to him long enough to find out."

"No, not long enough," Joan said. "But I don't think he had anything to do with that. It was probably the barbarian who returned for his ax. He probably came back a second time to find out more about us. It would be natural enough for him to be curious as to what we were like. Then, when I looked out of the hut and saw him, he decided to bring me here. He may have thought the newcomer, the mighty hunter, would be interested in me as a woman. Mighty hunters, men like gods, can be interested in women too."

"He seems to have been interested enough." Ames said. "But not in the way that barbarian thought, if you guessed right about him."

"If I could get my hands on that madman, there wouldn't be enough left of him to be interested in anything," Dorman said.

"You're being a little ungrateful for the way it turned out," Joan said. "If he'd been interested in me in a way that he wasn't, you'd have ten times as much reason for wanting to kill him. He struck me just once. It was a stinging blow, but my cheek isn't even swollen."

"That's beside the point," Dorman said. "If he was enraged enough to strike you, his viciousness wouldn't stop with that. What makes you think he wouldn't have gone on and raped you—if he hadn't been stopped. You can't be that naive."

"David's right," Ames said. "Tlacha's in just as much danger as long as we're imprisoned here and he stays alive. Killing him on sight should be our first order of business—if we run into him after rolling away that stone. The fact that he seems to be some kind of maniac makes him even more dangerous."

"I know," Dorman said, nodding. "Our other friends may be far less dangerous, despite their primitive aspect. The one who carried Joan off didn't harm her, and another came to her defense. They're not all like that, of course. The ones who kept jabbing at us on the walk we were forced to take were sadistic enough. And I'm not sure about the tall warrior. Your gesture of 'friendship' may have enraged him beyond endurance."

Tlacha spoke then, for the first time. "There may well be a nobleness in them," she said. "A few of them may be cruel, yes. How could it be otherwise, when they are as human as we are. But they live close to the good earth and they know how beautiful are the many bright lights in the sky and the changing seasons. They must change a little, even here. There are no flowers for them to cherish, but the snows can be just as beautiful. But they do not tear up the soil, or dream up ways of blowing the earth apart."

"There she goes again," Ames said. "It would do no good to remind her that we were once as they are. Or that their descendants will be exactly like us in the end."

"Not all of their descendants," Tlacha said. "There are millions of men and women on earth who still live close to the soil, or in the depths of the jungle. Why shouldn't they worship a mighty hunter as a god, mad though he may be? Oh, I know. It is perhaps wrong to slay animals, even for food. To destroy trees and flowers, if only for food.

"But they do very little and it is always a testing—of skill and courage, of one man against a mighty beast. Isn't it brave to be a great and invincible hunter? Why shouldn't he be worshipped as a god?"

"I could give you a half-dozen reasons," Ames said. "Your invincible hunter, Tlacha, can be a black-hearted scoundrel as well. He can be a homicidal maniac or a sane man with murder in his heart. You can't judge the nature of a man by just one thing he does well. I have nothing against the slaying of beasts otherwise."

"I have," Joan said. "I don't believe in the killing of animals for sport. But we've picked a very strange time to talk about what we do or do not believe. Our situation is terribly dangerous. We can at least agree about that."

"Look. We may have to make a drastic decision and we can't afford that kind of generosity, Tlacha, we can't give the enemy the benefit of any doubt. When it's kill or be killed—"

He stopped abruptly, gripped Dorman's arm and pointed toward the boulder-blocked opening that had been cut in the ice. The boulder was in motion, and was slowly but unmistakably being rolled back.

For a moment only a little light showed around it, then a great flood of sunlight streamed into the circular structure and the rough surface of the boulder vanished from sight.

Six tall warriors entered the hut, each stooping a little as they passed in turn through an entranceway that was three or four inches lower than their heads. They grouped themselves around its four occupants.

One of them spoke four words in Spanish that Dorman knew instantly had been learned from the bearded youth.

Roughly translated into English the four words were: "Come! It is time."

CHAPTER SIXTEEN

A fierce blaze of sunlight beat mercilessly down upon them, half-blinding them, and making the high, spectator-thronged ice terraces that towered above them seem to waver continuously back and forth. The terraces, eight or ten in number, completely encircled the enormous, ice-block structure into which they had been compelled to walk. The equally merciless proddings of the six warriors who had followed them into the structure continued until the warriors took up positions close to them at the base of the lowermost terrace.

The sun was almost directly overhead and some of the glare came from rays that were not deflected at all. But the light that was mirrored back from the snow and ice beneath their feet and high up on the ascending terraces was a great deal more dazzling. There was no way of shutting it out, because whenever they closed their eyes it seemed to burn through their eyelids into their brains.

There were thirty or forty warriors on each terrace, standing almost rigid, staring down with stone hatchets dangling from their arms.

Looking up, they could see only the warriors for a moment, enveloped in a shimmering haze. Then Ames touched Dorman lightly on the shoulder and pointed upwards toward a terrace that was occupied by a single figure, standing as rigid as the warriors with his arms folded across his chest.

Nothing about the bearded youth had changed. He was not clothed in fur, but was wearing the nondescript, somewhat tattered clothing of a poor Mexican fisherman, with a poncho draped over his shoulder—a poncho that had accompanied him into the cold waters of the Gulf when he had toppled, still furiously struggling with Dorman, from the rail of the capsizing boat.

Nothing about him had changed—not even the expression on his face. There was a look of madness in his eyes still, visible even from a distance and through the shimmering brightness. He was standing on the lowermost terrace, directly across from where Dorman was standing. The fact that it was the only otherwise empty terrace pointed up his isolation in quite a startling way, giving him the look of a lean, almost vulturine bird of prey poised on the brink of a precipice and about to go winging down toward some moving object that had caught its eye.

Quite suddenly there was a stir of movement behind Dorman and he saw, without more than half-turning, that the six warriors were moving away from him. Moving away from Ames, Tlacha and Joan as well, in the direction of the entrance to the ice-block structure through which they had come.

He turned about completely then but before he could call Ames' attention to the change that had taken place behind them, the warriors had vanished and they were alone.

There was something else that neither Dorman or Ames had been aware of until that moment. There was a long, twenty-foot-high aperture between the smooth surface of ice on which they were standing and the lowermost terrace. And out of that opening, something was now swiftly emerging that glistened in the sunlight—something scaly and huge that was either crawling or heaving itself up out of a cavernous darkness into full view of the warrior spectators.

It took the creature no more than a few seconds to emerge, and start crossing the ice toward Ames. It was crossing toward Dorman, Joan and Tlacha as well, but more directly toward Ames, who had taken three or four quick steps forward on catching sight of it.

It was a gigantic, snow-white lizard, almost as large as the first of the three slain beasts that they had encountered. Now, quite suddenly, a loud, rhythmic drumming began again, from high up on one of the terraces.

It had seemed incredible to Dorman that Ames had been allowed to keep the great bow strapped to his shoulder, that it had not been taken from him even during his imprisonment, when it would have been of great value if they had somehow managed to roll the boulder back. It had even made him wonder if even the warriors had not been a little mad.

But now he could see that there had been a method in their madness. To have taken the bow away and given it back to Ames before the emergence of the beast would have alerted him to the danger almost instantly. It would have kept him from being taken by surprise, and robbed a cruel spectator sport of a breathless moment of suspense, when Ames' quickness of mind and hand would be more important than the bow itself.

Dorman heard Tlacha cry out in alarm, and swung about to make sure that she would not lose her head and rush to Ames' side. Joan was standing very still, her eyes on the swiftly advancing reptile. But Tlacha had already begun to move, and Dorman had to plant himself directly in front of her and gesture her back.

The great bow was in Ames' hand now and he was drawing an arrow from the quiver at his waist. He notched the bowstring into the arrow, took a quick step backwards and raised the bow until the arrow was pointing directly at the scaly monster's head.

There was a sharp, vibrant *twang* as the arrow left the bow.

The gigantic reptile was within thirty feet of Ames when the arrow thudded into the middle of its scaly throat, causing it to rear up with what sounded like a rasping intake of breath.

Somehow the sound was more chilling than the full-throated roar of a wounded lion or tiger would have been. It remained for a moment almost vertical, with its claw-tipped forelimbs flailing the air. Then it descended on all fours and continued to advance.

Ames had retreated several feet, but the beast was almost upon him again when another arrow found its mark, this time directly between the scaly monster's eyes.

He could hardly have scored a more direct hit, in a more vital spot. But the beast advanced now in a flying leap, the two arrows quivering in its flesh.

One of its forelimbs lashed out and struck Ames across the chest, hurling him to the ice as it went plunging past

him to land on its feet thirty feet away. It reared up again,
swaying back and forth and began to turn slowly about.

Ames was not getting up. He lay in a crumpled heap on
the ice, the great bow two yards distant from him, the
quiver twisted sharply beneath him, with just one arrow
protruding.

The gigantic reptile was not moving back toward him.
It had turned almost completely about and was moving in
the direction of Joan and Tlacha. It had fallen to all fours
again and appeared to be close to death, for its long body
was trembling convulsively. This should have slowed its
advance across the ice, but no uninjured beast could have
suddenly moved more swiftly.

It had been moving also in the direction of Dorman.
But only for an instant, for it had taken Dorman barely
five seconds to get to where Ames was lying, and pick up
the bow. He freed the protruding arrow with a quick, upward jerk, inserted it, and drew the bowstring taut,
straightening as he did so.

He took careful aim, the bow at shoulder level. Although he had never taken aim with a great bow before
and it seemed suddenly much larger and heavier than it
actually was, the arrow left it with as vibrant a *twang* as
the one which Ames had sent speeding toward the scaly
monster's throat.

The great lizard had reared again, and it was not at its
throat that Dorman had aimed, but at where he hoped its
sluggishly beating heart would be located.

Nothing mattered now but the way the great lizard was
crumpling, and relief swept over him when he saw that it
had come to an abrupt halt.

He would not have believed that so enormous a beast,
armored and cold-blooded and quite different from a
mammal, could have died so instantly if he had not
watched it happen.

The beast did not move at all after it crashed down on
the ice, did not so much as twitch. It simply crashed down
and lay still.

The drums on the uppermost terraces had continued to
beat throughout the entire spectacle, even when the war-

riors must have known it was not turning out as they could have wished. But suddenly the rhythmic beating stopped and a voice shouted in Spanish three words that none of the warriors would have needed to learn, for it was the bearded youth himself who shouted them.

Roughly translated, the three words were: "Release another beast."

CHAPTER SEVENTEEN

Tlacha had darted past the slain, crumpled beast and was now at Ames' side, bending over him. At first Dorman thought that her only concern was to find out how badly he had been injured. He had no doubt at all that that was her chief concern. But when he saw that she was fumbling with the folds of his outer skin, drawing them apart, he began to wonder if some sudden madness had not come upon her.

He stood very still, too startled for an instant to move to where she was crouching. It was only when her hands came out from beneath the furskin, holding Ames' pistol —she seemed to need both hands just to raise it—and turned about to face the terrace where the bearded youth was standing that Dorman began to understand her intentions.

He was suddenly very sure when she got slowly to her feet, and raised the pistol—still with both hands—until the heavy weapon was pointing directly at the youth.

She fired the gun without seeming to know exactly how to aim it, content with just keeping it pointed, as accurately as she could, at the spot where the youth was standing.

The roar of the long-barreled pistol was deafening.

For an instant Dorman's only thought was how dangerous and uncertain the recoil of so large a gun could be in the hands of so tiny a woman. He did not even know at what precise instant the bearded youth began to crumple, for when he raised his eyes he was no longer on the terrace. All Dorman saw was a flash of motion, and then the youth was lying spreadeagled on the ice at the base of the lowermost terrace, with a dull red stain on his crumpled poncho.

Tlacha gave a stricken sob, and covered her face with her hands. The pistol had dropped to the ice and it was Dorman who picked it up as he rushed to support her,

123

half-expecting to see her collapse before he could get to her.

"I thought he was far away, in Yucatan," she said, shivering. "I knew, when I saw him, that his poor brain had— Oh, I want to die. Help me to die. It was not my brother's fault that he was born proud, with memories of a vanished greatness."

"Your brother. You didn't know—"

"Not until I saw him."

Ames had begun to stir a little and Dorman bent quickly, thrusting both of his hands under Ames' armpits and tried to raise him. For an instant it seemed hopeless, and then, quite suddenly, Ames was getting up of his own accord. More of his strength seemed to return even as he rose and he seemed aware of what Dorman was trying to tell him.

"We've got to try to get out before they—"

Dorman couldn't go on, because he'd forgotten what he had started to say. He could hear Joan's voice trying to say something to Ames too—or was it Tlacha she was pleading with. He could feel a tugging at his arm—the old, old tugging that had become so familiar to him, that always seemed to bring Joan closer to him—and then—and then—

Everything about him seemed to be dissolving in a gray mist and there were strange images again, passing before him as if in separate frames. Plains of snow and ice and then plains that were not snow-covered at all, and stunted trees with birds that could have been ravens or crows circling about high in the sky, and then just plains of grass, a green land golden in the dying day, and a return of what looked like the start of a jungle—

It was a long time—or perhaps a short time, how could he really know?—when all of the landscapes and all of the frame vanished, and he found himself staring incredulously at Joan across a wide expanse of shining sand. She was waving to him and looking a little stunned. Then she had gotten to her feet and was running straight toward him, her hair blowing in the wind.

EPILOGUE

The hospital corridor was gray and dismal and silent, as hospital corridors usually are. It could have been in New York or Chicago or Los Angeles. But it wasn't. It was in Mexico City and the nurses whom Dorman and Joan passed on their way to Ames' room glanced at them with a little more of a 'siesta-calm' look in their eyes than if the hospital had been in New York or Chicago or Los Angeles. But otherwise there was no difference at all.

Ames was sitting up in bed when they entered the room and shut the door firmly behind them and Tlacha was standing at his side. There were flowers on a table at the foot of the bed, which was no more than what one would have expected to find.

They remained for a moment smiling down at him and he smiled back. Then a more serious look came into his eyes. "Well, what have you decided the answer is?" he asked. "Or haven't you made up your minds?"

"We've both given it a great deal of thought," Dorman told him. "I'm convinced—and Joan agrees with me—that there *was* some kind of time shift, beyond any possibility of doubt. When the beast came up out of the earth—and there seems to have been two of them—the energies it carried with it were so tremendous that it shook, as I believe I said once before, the very keystone of matter itself. It shook the space-time continuum as well and we wavered back through time."

"*Wavered* is good," Ames said. "On the magnetic wave principle perhaps."

"It could have been something like that. But it didn't last. It wore off and we 'wavered' back."

"It couldn't have happened at a more fortunate time," Ames said. "Our warrior friends would have put both their stone axes and their spears to practical use—from their point of view."

"I'm afraid they would have," Dorman said.

125

Ames was silent for a moment. Then he said: "Where do you suppose the two beasts are now? What became of them? Are they still back in the Ice Age?"

"I don't think so," Dorman said. "I don't think they belonged in that world any more than we did. They probably wavered back too—to where they came from."

"Then you still believe there may be prehistoric monsters still surviving deep within the earth, changed through long ages of evolutionary adaptation into animals with the ability to generate billions of electron volts?"

"I don't know," Dorman said. "If there is such a hollow world it must be overlaid with millions of tons of closer-to-the-surface rocks or those beasts would have emerged more often. There may be a few vents, needing an earthquake or a man-made cataclysm to widen them sufficiently to enable the beasts to escape. The hollow world, if it exists, may be very close to the earth's iron core."

"And if it doesn't exist?"

"The beasts could have come from some other dimension of space-time. But that seems unlikely, since they came up out of the ground, after a man-made cataclysm. And we mustn't forget the Toltec legends, dating back more than a thousand years."

"Yes . . . well, all I can say is I hope it doesn't happen again, at least in our lifetime."

"That's a very selfish thing to say," Tlacha said, smiling.

"All men have a selfish side to their natures, Tlacha," Joan said. "And most women."

"There's one thing that still puzzles me," Ames said. "Actually, it staggers me. If we wavered back, as you say, why did you and Joan find yourselves on the beach you left when you went out in the fishing boat to get a closer look at the monster? If you wavered back to exactly where you were when the light swirled over you, why weren't you swimming in the Gulf? And why did Tlacha and I find ourselves about seven miles from her father's land?"

"If we passed back into the past through some distortion of the space-time continuum," Dorman said, "the same distortion—the time we spent in the Glacial Age—could have brought us back in a slightly different location."

"That's one thing, at least, that we can be thankful for," Ames said.

When they left the hospital room and were walking back along the corridor, Dorman found himself a little angry.

"Just one thing to be thankful for!" he said. "He'll feel differently about it in another week, when he's completely over the blow that lizard delivered—just before I sent an arrow into it."

"You mean *we've* more than just one thing to be thankful for?" Joan asked.

"Not exactly. But it's such a big thing; he had no right to speak of it in that way. He must feel the same way about Tlacha as I do about you."

"I know what you mean," Joan said.